Hindsight's a funny thing, isn't it? For instance, with the benefit of hindsight, I can keep replaying the first time I ever asked a girl out – Karen, one of the It girls from my class – and think of, ooh, twenty cleverer, funnier things that I *could* have said to charm her into fancying me. Then there was the time I decided it'd be good fun to roll down a hill in shorts without noticing that the bottom bit was really steep and covered in nettles – I *definitely* wouldn't do that again. And with hindsight, I probably shouldn't have touched the Ginger Psycho, because he took that as his cue to punch me in the face. Quite hard, actually.

Also available in this series:

Going Out with a Bang
They Think it's all Over

Coming soon:

The not so Great Outdoors

Another almost-true story by Dylan Douglas (age 13)

Itching for a Fight

Joel Snape

SCHOLASTIC

Scholastic Children's Books,
Commonwealth House, 1–19 New Oxford Street,
London, WC1A 1NU, UK
a division of Scholastic Ltd
London ~ New York ~ Toronto ~ Sydney ~ Auckland
Mexico City ~ New Delhi ~ Hong Kong

First published in the UK by Scholastic Ltd, 2005

ISBN 0 439 95966 7

Printed and bound by Nørhaven Paperback A/S, Denmark

10 9 8 7 6 5 4 3 2 1

To Neil, Lucy, Salvo and everyone else who's taught me that martial arts instructors aren't all *psycho.*

And thanks to Amanda and Jane, who are just lovely.

Make Like a Banana and . . . Split!

"Aooooow!" yelped Dec, rolling around on the floor.

I sighed and turned the volume up on the TV. This was all Jean-Claude Van Damme's fault.

Don't get me wrong. It wasn't as if Jean-Claude had turned up at my best mate's nice, flowery wallpapered house in the suburbs of Bristol and whacked Dec in the jaw personally. I doubt that Jean-Claude even knows where Bristol is – and even if he *did*, I doubt he'd take time out of his busy face-punching schedule to drop by and spinning-kick a thirteen year old. It's just that. . . Well, I probably ought to explain a bit first.

The good thing about having a bigger brother like mine is, when he eventually leaves home, you sort of inherit all his stuff by default. CDs, books, comics, that cool little alarm clock that plays the theme tune from *The Simpsons* – none of it's strictly *yours*, but if it somehow finds its way into your room, he's not exactly going to notice on one of his bi-monthly laundry trips home, is he? At first you're just borrowing it, then it starts to get lost in the clutter of your own collection of stuff, then – after about three months – I reckon it becomes officially yours. Squatter's rights, see?

Anyway, this is especially good news for me, because Lennon's got one of the finest collections of terrible videos known to man. Horror films, kung-fu films, cheesy action films – Lennon's stash might not have many period dramas, but if you want to see someone's head exploding, it's the only place to go. The downside is, my mum doesn't exactly approve of it. She's OK with a bit of harmless shooting, maybe even the occasional stabbing, but zombies getting chopped to bits with a hedge-strimmer? Forget it. Which is why it's good to have a mate like Dec.

Dec's mum and dad always seem to be out – at dinner parties, concerts, or whatever posh parents do together – which means that, if you want to settle down on Sunday and watch a samurai killing ninja assassins with a booby-trapped pram (or whatever), Dec's horrible paisley living room's the place to go.

"Aaaaowww," Dec carried on, dropping into more of a low moan. I would have helped, but it had taken me a good half-hour to get into a comfortable groove on the sofa, and I didn't want to let all that hard work go to waste.

See, the trouble started because, let's face it, you can guarantee that Jean-Claude's going to do at least three things in all of his films:

1) A spinning kick. This is self-explanatory. He usually pulls it out against the final bad guy, who doesn't see it coming despite the fact that it seems to take about half an hour to do.

2) He gets his bum out. We're a bit mystified about why Jean-Claude does this – his films can't get *that* many female viewers – but he definitely ends up dropping his trousers a lot. Maybe he's just proud of it – it *is* quite tanned.

But, most importantly:

3) He does the splits. He does this all the time. It's like sometimes he does it for a good reason –

like dodging low-flying bullets or dropping down low enough to smack someone in the unmentionables. Sometimes he just does it to show off. But he *always* does it.

And he makes it look really easy. Which is where the trouble began.

"Owwww!" went Dec again, interrupting my train of thought.

"Dec," said Will. "You're spoiling the film."

To be honest, I'd sort of lost interest in the film. It was the bit where Jean-Claude was getting his head kicked in – which, as everyone knows, always comes just before he gets his second wind and batters the other person senseless. Nope, I was more interested in whether my best mate – who'd tried dropping into the splits without even bothering to warm up – was going to be able to walk properly by the time his mum got home. Fortunately, he seemed to be recovering.

"Yeah, like *you* could do any better than that," he said, rolling into a sitting position and swatting Will around the back of the head.

"Like I'd be stupid enough to *try*," huffed Will, swinging an arm behind him in the vague direction of Dec's voice and missing him completely.

Jean-Claude had moved on to the bit where the other person stops blocking and lets himself get repeatedly punched in the face. Next up: the bit where Jean-Claude beats the bad guy and lets him live, only to be forced to kill him when he gets attacked from behind. *Bo-rring.* The Will/Dec confrontation was much more interesting.

"Go on," Dec was saying to the back of Will's head, "hit me in the stomach. I'll tense up. Bet you can't even punch properly."

"Don't be daft," Will was saying, still trying to concentrate on the TV, "that's how Houdini died."

"Hah!" Dec seemed to have regained the use of his legs, which he was now using to dance around Will, zinging the occasional shadow-boxing-style punch *just* close enough to his head to be annoying. "You'd never hit me, anyway. Float like a butterfly, sting like a bee!"

"Right!" shouted Will. Jean-Claude had finished off his opponent, which seemed to be the cue for action. He dived at Dec, who flipped him over easily . . . and sat on him. Hmm. I wondered why Jean-Claude never did that.

"Told you," said a triumphant Dec, giving Will a gentle pummelling in the ribs.

"Gedddofff!" shouted Will, trying to shove Dec away.

"Stay down. . ." said Dec, wagging a finger and doing a really terrible impression of Jean-Claude's Belgian accent, "and live."

Will, it seemed, wasn't too bothered about threats – he just wanted to get up. After a bit more thrashing about, he finally managed to grab a cushion off the sofa . . . and smash Dec in the head with it.

"Oww!" yelped Dec, grabbing a cushion of his own. "I *warned* you. . ."

He swatted Will's feeble attempts at blocking aside, pinned his arms with his knees and started rhythmically bashing him in the face with the cushion.

". . .you *don't* mess. . ."

Bash.

". . .with the best. . ."

Bash.

". . .because the best. . ."

Bash.

". . .don't *mess.*"

BASH.

And, of course, that was when Dec's parents walked in.

When the Going Gets Tofu...

"I'm ho-ome!" I shouted, slamming the front door and keeping my ears open for sounds of life from my family.

The *other* thing about Dec's mum and dad is, they don't seem to care *what* he gets up to. In my house, the scene that greeted them when they arrived home would've provoked a ten-minute lecture including the words "best cushions" "could've *broken* something" "aren't you a bit old" and so on, and so on. Dec's mum just huffed a little "Oh for heaven's *sake*" and swept out of the room, leaving Will and me to say our (slightly embarrassed) goodbyes. Yeah, I envy the fact that Dec never seems to get in trouble, but it must be weird to *never* get shouted at. Not a problem I ever have.

"Shut up!" hissed my sister Becky, leaning around the kitchen door.

"Inspectors?"

"Yep."

"Sorry."

My mum's a teacher. Not at my school (well, not since I was at junior school, anyway, which was a *major* relief, let me tell you) but at the junior school just down the road. But, as she never gets tired of telling anyone who even *dares* mention being jealous of "all that holiday", it's not as easy as you think. There are lesson plans to do, reports to write, tests to mark, meetings to turn up at – just doing all that seems to keep her busy until about three hours after all the little kids go home. And, like all teachers, my mum gets *especially* upset whenever the education secretary (whoever *that* is) talks about "falling standards" or any of that stuff. And *this* fortnight was going to be *especially* stressful, because it was one of those times when The Inspectors were in school, poking about in lessons and generally making all the teachers super-stressed. Becky waved in the direction of the living room, where my mum was sitting with bits of paper and books scattered all over the table.

"I'm making the tea tonight," explained Becky. "*She's* stressing out."

"Oh, great," I groaned.

"It's nice of Becky to offer, Dylan," interrupted Mum, walking into the kitchen and using the voice that makes the eight year olds in her class go silent. "And it wouldn't hurt you to help out once in a while."

"He can wash up, if he wants to help," Becky joined in, "I'm meeting someone later."

"Brilliant," I groaned, again.

It's not that I've got anything against my sister's cooking, by the way. She's a lot better at it than me – although, considering that my repertoire consists mostly of sandwiches and mashed potato, that isn't too hard. And she's definitely a *lot* better than my brother Lennon, whose idea of a filling meal's his soon-to-be-patented baked bean pasta. (Want the recipe? Make some pasta, mash up some Heinz beans and tip them over the top – he's not exactly Jamie Oliver.) It's just that, since she turned vegetarian a couple of years ago, everything Becky makes has some sort of horrible meat-substitute in it. And it's always a nightmare trying to scrape it off the pan afterwards.

"What're we having?" I said, trying to look enthusiastic.

Becky flashed me a dirty look and said: "Tofu and spinach." Proving my point beautifully.

"Sounds *lovely*," I said, peering into the wok she was holding, full of what looked like leaves and slices of rubber. "Mmm. Yum."

"What?" Becky gave me another look.

"Nothing," I said, backing out of the kitchen without breaking eye contact.

"Looking forward to dinner?" I groaned, flopping on to the living room sofa.

"What? Oh. . ." My dad looked up from his latest project – reorganizing his albums according to some obscure system nobody else can understand. "Well, it's nice of Becky to help."

He grinned at me. We both knew what *that* meant – if my dad was in charge of making the tea, we'd all be eating prawn crackers and crispy duck from the local takeaway. When she gets in a nostalgic mood, Mum *loves* telling us all about how Dad lived on beans on toast for the first six months she knew him – his idea of a romantic night out was splurging on haddock and chips. Dad winked.

"And I'm sure whatever she's making's going to be *lovely.*"

"Yeah," I groaned. "I'm sure. . ."

"This is . . . interesting, Becky," said my dad, prodding his tofu with a fork. He didn't seem to be eating it so much as moving it around.

"Mmmf," I agreed. Tofu wasn't so bad, as long as you dunked it in so much soy sauce that you couldn't actually *taste* it. That was tricky too, of course, because you had to chew each lump for at least twenty seconds before you could even have a go at swallowing it.

Fortunately, though, I was *just* at a gap between chews when the phone rang.

"I'll get it!" I yelped, hoping it was Will, Dec, or some other sort of distraction that I could use until the tofu was forgotten. As it turned out, I was half-right.

"Evening, Dylan," said Lennon, sounding chirpy, "I've just broken my wrist."

"What?" I said. "How?"

"Accident," said Lennon – as if he'd have done it on purpose. "Look, can I talk to you?"

"Who is it, Dylan?" shouted Becky from the kitchen.

"Lennon," I called back.

"Oh, good," Mum called, her voice brightening up. "I've been trying to get hold of him all week."

"Expecting a call?" I smirked at Becky as I slid back into my seat.

"*No,*" said Becky, furiously digging into her tofu.

I probably wouldn't have let it drop there – something about the shade of red Becky seemed to be turning suggested it wasn't just a result of soy sauce. But, unfortunately, that was exactly the moment we all heard Mum's voice rising as she squeaked: "You've done WHAAAT?"

Good old Lennon.

Just Browsing, Thanks

"Yes. . . Yes. . . Maybe. . . No. . . No. . . Eurgh, definitely not. . ." Dec was muttering to himself, scanning the Virgin Megastore's CD racks.

"Like they'd be interested *anyway*," I pointed out, grumpily.

"What?"

"Nothing."

The thing is, when *most* people go record shopping, I'm pretty sure they base the albums they look at on which songs they like. Not Dec – nope. He bases his buying decisions on exactly two things: how much he fancies the singers, and whether there's a free copy of their video included on their CD. Obviously, he's not a big fan of The Darkness.

"Whatever. . ." Dec turned back to the Chart

rack. "Yes, but only when she's wearing that really short skirt. . ."

Sigh. To be honest, I can't really see what the attraction of going out with a pop star is *anyway.* Well, OK, I *can,* but just picture it – every time you went on a date, you'd have photographers from *Heat* taking snaps of you both, then writing, "Beyoncé – pictured here with Loser Nobody Boyfriend" in the captions. And you wouldn't be able to go to Maccy D's, because you'd get mobbed, and she wouldn't be able to eat anything except cucumbers and tomatoes anyway. And – worst of all – you'd have half of the country's teen skateboarding population drooling over pictures of her. Nope, I think I'd be much better off with somebody a bit more normal – like, say, *Kate.* Ah, Kate. She's been in my class for nearly four months now, and she's funny and nice and probably prettier than half of the people in the charts anyway, and we're sort of mates, but . . . well. . .

"See, those two're lovely, but why can't they just get rid of *her?*" Dec said, interrupting my thoughts and pointing at a Sugababe who – I'm pretty sure – wouldn't be all that heartbroken to hear that Dec doesn't fancy her.

"Because she's the best singer," I explained, slightly impatiently. "Are you nearly finished in here?"

"Nope – haven't even looked at the posters yet." Dec smirked, wandering off towards the back of the shop.

Sigh. I absent-mindedly picked up a CD and half-read the tedious-sounding song titles on the back. It wasn't as if I could afford to be buying albums anyway – I'd only really come into town to avoid my increasingly stressed-out mum and permanently stress-promoting sister. Why did she have to be such a freak? Why couldn't she just eat burgers like anyone normal? And, come to think of it, why hadn't she been awake when I left the house in the morn—

"Thinking of buying that?" came a female voice.

"Just looking, thanks." I turned round, half-expecting to have to fend off a pushy, pimply shop assistant who had me pegged as a potential shoplifter. And then I saw who it was. "I . . . um . . . really respect her musical talent."

"Really?" asked Kate, giving me a smile that I can only really call "twinkly". "That wouldn't have anything to do with her last video, would it?"

As embarrassing moments go, this had to be somewhere just behind watching *Titanic* with my gran and remembering – too late – that Kate Winslet takes her top off about halfway through. Let's just say you wouldn't be able to describe the video Kate had just reminded me of without the word "jiggling" featuring pretty heavily.

"No, apparently she writes her own songs," I lied, joke-defensively. "And she's, um, got a nice hat."

"Riiiight," said Kate, rolling her eyes.

"Well, who do *you* like?" I half-demanded, giving her a quick smile.

"Ummm. . ." said Kate, suddenly looking flustered and scanning the racks for somebody a) worth listening to and b) not too obviously good-looking, ". . .him?"

"You're *joking,*" I said. "He's really whiny. *And* he's got a neck like a walrus."

"Yeah, well at least he's got a nice smile," said Kate, grinning back at me and pointing at another album cover belonging to someone whose, um, "musical ability" I'm a big fan of. "Apparently *she's* got so much botox injected into her face she can hardly move it."

"Yeah?" I said, pointing at a pop star with his shirt flapping open to expose a perfectly toned and tanned washboard stomach. "Well, apparently *his* six-pack's made of plastic. He probably can't go on a plane without his stomach exploding."

"Well, it couldn't make him any worse at singing," said Kate, still smiling. "How are you, Dylan?"

"Um, OK," I said. I thought it was a sign of progress that I was joking around and being this casual. I mean, normally when I talk to girls I fancy, I'm a stuttering, jittery wreck.

"I'm glad I saw you, actually," said Kate. "Um, what're you doing a week on Friday?"

"Friday?" I repeated. *Beeeeoooww*, went my brain. *We are experiencing technical difficulties.* Was Kate about to ask me out on a . . . date? "I, um, don't think I'm doing anything. Why?"

Nice one, genius, went my brain. *Like you ever do anything on a Friday. Playing it cool, are you?*

"Ah, no reason. . ." said Kate, smiling again. "Just don't plan anything, OK?"

"Come on, you can tell me. . ." I coaxed, trying to give her my best charming look.

"We-eellll. . ." said Kate, giving me a look. "I suppose I *could*. . ."

"Mate, you've *got* to come and look at this poster of Christina Aguilera!" interrupted Dec. "You can almost see her – oh, hi Kate!"

"Hi Dec," said Kate. "Look, Dylan, I'll talk to you later, OK? Byee!"

And she was gone, giving us a little wave as she disappeared through the crush of Sunday shoppers.

"Sorry, mate, didn't cramp your style there, did I?"

"No. . ." I mumbled, but I was busy wondering two completely different things:

a) What did Kate want? And. . .

b) How many CDs would I send flying if I tried to take Dec out with a Jean-Claude-style spinning kick?

That'll Leave a Mark...

Drrreee . . . der . . . der . . . der, came the tinny little ringing noise from Dec's pocket. I pretended not to notice.

It was Monday evening. It was the end of a fair-to-middling day at school, with only the usual input from the Idiots (Keith melted one of my pens during chemistry), and very little hassle from teachers (I used the old "yep, it's just in my. . . Oh, no! I've left it at home!" homework bluff on nice old Mrs Quitely, who didn't mind at all), but now I had to put up with this.

Der . . . da-da . . . der-dum-da-da.

"So what did your brother actually *do* to his arm?" asked Dec, as if he couldn't hear the tune coming from his trousers.

"Dunno," I said. "My mum spoke to him. He

just said something about being drunk. So, obviously she panicked and now she's off to see him at the weekend."

Der-der-der-der-der-der! Now it was obvious – it was definitely something or other by Eminem making Dec's trousers rumble, although without any lyrics over the top, it sounded a lot like a random series of bleeps.

"Are you going to answer that?" I asked.

"What?" said Dec, innocently.

It was driving me mad. Honestly, I think Dec spends more time fiddling about with ringtones than he actually spends on the phone. This one had managed a week, which had to be some sort of record.

Der-der-der-der. . .

The phone went back to the start of the theme, and just before I could strangle Dec, he yanked it out of his pocket, looked at the display, frowned and made a little "tch" noise.

Der-der-der-der. . .

"Just *answer* it." I was practically pleading now.

"Can't."

"Why not?"

"Pffft."

Dec shrugged, and made a little face like he

was almost *insulted* by the fact that the mystery caller was hassling him on his own phone. Eventually, it stopped, and Dec put it carefully back in his pocket. We carried on walking for a bit, not saying anything.

"Don't you want to know who that was?" asked Dec. I *knew* he'd crack first.

"Not particularly," I said. Might as well draw it out a bit.

"Course you do."

"Meh." I shrugged.

"Fine," said Dec. "I won't tell you, then."

"Fine."

"Good."

We carried on walking for about three seconds. Then, Dec started again.

"It was this girl I met a couple of weeks ago."

Honestly, this is why Dec'd be such a bad criminal. The police could just go a bit quiet and he'd collapse and tell them about all his diamond robberies just to sound cool.

"Yeah? Where'd you meet her?" I said, keeping up the casual front. Obviously, finding out that Dec was being pestered by a girl who didn't even go to our school was actually pretty interesting, but if Dec *knew* I cared, he'd drag it out for as long as humanly possible.

"Skatepark." Dec shrugged. "She gave me a Hula Hoop."

Typical. The longer Dec spends at the skatepark, the less time he seems to spend actually skating. He's more of an expert in sitting on the grassy hill next to it, cadging crisps off unsuspecting girls who're impressed by his scuff-free skateboard.

"Why didn't you tell me?"

"Meh." Oops. I'd obviously been a bit too keen – now it was Dec's turn to be disinterested. We both went silent, then Dec piped up again.

"She's *mental,*" he said. "I spent, like, one *day* hanging out with her and stuff, and now she keeps ringing me *all the time.* It's like having a *stalker.*"

I thought about that for a second – it didn't sound all that bad. I mean, I wouldn't want someone following me around and going through my rubbish, or whatever stalkers do, but somebody – some *girl* – ringing you up all the time? I hate to admit it, but that actually sounded quite nice. Obviously, I didn't admit any of that to Dec.

"So when're you going to ring her back?" I said, instead.

"What?" said Dec. "I'm not." Although it almost sounded like he wanted to add ". . .you idiot" to the end of that bit. "She wants to hang out with me *all the time.* I can't handle that, mate, I'm just not going to answer her calls. She'll get the message."

"That's not all that nice, is it?" I said, knowing how weedy I sounded.

"So?" said Dec, sounding even *more* like he wanted to call me an idiot. "Dylan, you're too nice."

"What?" I said. Surely being too nice is like being *too* clever, or *too* happy – it just can't happen.

"It's like with Kate," he carried on, in his best lecturing voice. "You've been mates with her for too long, and now you're in the friendship circle."

"No, no, no. I'm not in the friendship circle," I protested, not really knowing what the friendship circle was.

"Mate, you are," Dec said, looking exasperated. "You're like back-up. You're the standby. You're the nice mate she's going to come running to when. . ." He trailed off.

"When what?" I asked, keen to hear the rest of this insane theory.

"Oh ——" Dec said a word that I'm not going to repeat here, just in case my mum reads this.

"What?" I said. Then I saw what he was looking at.

Three kids were sauntering towards us. I didn't recognize any of them, but I recognized their uniform – the light-blue shirt and dark-blue tie combo meant they had to be from Lowfield.

"Oh ——" I said a word that was just about as bad as Dec's.

I should probably explain.

Lowfield's the *other* school near my house. Everyone knows someone who knows someone who goes there, but nobody seems to know what it's *really* like. I mean, if you believed *all* the rumours, virtually everyone at Lowfield either:

a) Sniffed glue.

b) Had a GCSE in shoplifting.

or:

c) Set fire to cats.

To be honest, I'm not sure I believe *any* of

that, but Lowfield's definitely got a bit of a reputation. Enough of a reputation, in fact, for my mum and dad to decide it'd be worth the extra twenty minutes' walk to get to our school, rather than risking me turning into some sort of Pritt-stick-addicted shoplifter. And enough of a reputation that, when you saw some Lowfield kids coming in the opposite direction, you usually crossed the road. The trouble was, we'd left it too late – these Lowfield kids were right on top of us, and at that range, running's like being the injured wildebeest in a nature documentary – you're just going to attract the attention of predators. Besides which, these particular Lowfield lads weren't just ambling along on our side of the road – they were heading straight for us.

"Look at this. . ." said the tallest of the Lowfield kids, who was also the thinnest – and the one with the most acne. Honestly, he looked like he'd just been whacked in the face with a meat-feast pizza. The other thing I couldn't help noticing was his huge Adam's apple – it seemed to have a life of its own, even though he'd only said about three words, and it carried on bobbing as he kept talking.

"Shouldn't you girls be holding hands?"

I shuffled uncomfortably, but didn't say anything. In fact, the only person who made any noise at all was the shorter, wider Lowfield lad to Pizza Boy's right. It wasn't like a laugh, really, more like a sort of snuffly, grunty noise to show that he thought Pizza Boy was being funny.

"All right, mate?" Dec said, sidestepping on to the grass to let the Lowfield boys past. Unfortunately, they just decided to spread out and stop instead. The third member of the posse, the one who hadn't made a sound yet, was just staring at us, really intensely. Everything about him was wiry, from his arms and legs right up to his hair, which was about the colour of that copper wire you make mini-electromagnets out of. He was just *staring* at Dec, with creepy, baby-blue eyes locked on to my best mate. And he seemed to be turning that shade of red that you normally see in cartoon characters with steam coming out of their ears. The other two just looked like your typical bullies, but he looked like a psycho.

"I'm not your mate, pal," hissed Pizza Boy, while Ginger Psycho carried on staring. I stared intently at a bush just past his head. To be honest, I couldn't remember whether you were supposed to make eye contact with nutcases or not. I think I remember once reading that you're not supposed to look directly at an angry bear. Or was that gorillas?

Unfortunately, I didn't have time to think about what Steve "Crocodile Hunter" Irwin would do with a Ginger Psycho, because at about that point, things started to happen quite quickly. Ginger Psycho, looking like he'd made his decision, half-lunged towards Dec, Dec hid behind *me*, and I did the stupidest thing humanly possible.

"Look," I said, in my calmest voice, grabbing Ginger Psycho's shoulder. "Let's just calm down, shall we?"

Hindsight's a funny thing, isn't it? For instance, with the benefit of hindsight, I can keep replaying the first time I ever asked a girl out – Karen, one of the It girls from my class – and think of, ooh, twenty cleverer, funnier things that I *could* have said to charm her into fancying me. Then there was the time I decided it'd be good fun to roll down a hill in shorts without noticing that the bottom bit was really steep and covered in nettles – I *definitely* wouldn't do that again. And with hindsight, I probably shouldn't have touched the Ginger Psycho, because he took that as his cue to punch me in the face. Quite hard, actually.

Black, Blue and a Little Bit Green...

"Are you OK?" asked Dec, which seemed to be in second place behind "Did that hurt?" in the list of Stupid Questions To Ask Someone Who's Just Been Punched In The Face.

I mean, I *was* bending over and clutching my cheek – what did he think I was doing it for?

"What do you think?" I asked, slightly bitterly – and then, maybe a *bit* unfairly, added, "Why didn't he hit *you*? You're the one he was staring at."

"Dunno. It's OK, they've gone now," Dec said quickly, trying to cheer me up.

"Brilliant," I said. "Maybe I hurt him and he's gone home to put an elastoplast on his knuckles."

I doubted that, though. Although I couldn't

really remember the punch properly – it was just like a little flash of pain and then a numb sort of feeling – I definitely remembered what happened afterwards, even though I could only rely on my ears. Dec made a weak little protest noise, Pizza Boy laughed, Grunty grunted, and Ginger Psycho just said something like, "I'll see you later, *mate.*" And no, it hadn't sounded like I'd managed to fracture his hand with my iron-hard cheekbone.

"Come on, let's have a look," Dec insisted, trying to prise my hand away from my eye. "It's probably not that ba. . ."

"*What?*" I said, bringing my hand back up to my face and giving the general area around it an experimental prod. *Ouch.*

"Nothing," said Dec, although his shocked expression wasn't exactly filling me with confidence. "Anyway, do you know who that *was*? The one who punched you?"

"Nope," I said, blinking back the tears that were still coming out of my eye. "My first guess would've been Mike Tyson, but he hasn't got ginger hair."

"That was Gary Pierce," said Dec. I blinked some more. "*Gary Pierce,*" he said again, obviously feeling that I wasn't impressed enough by the name. "He's one of the hardest lads at Lowfield. He's an absolute nutter. I heard he once punched one of the *teachers*."

"Right." I winced. That was actually sort of comforting – I mean, imagine getting beaten up by one of the *wimpiest* lads at Lowfield. You'd never live it down. "Anyway, how come *you* know so much about him?"

"Well, erm, *everyone's* heard of him, you know?" Dec said, quickly. "Anyway, we should probably steer clear of him in future."

"You think?" I asked, doing the best "Duh" expression I could – which wasn't very good, considering that I still had to hold on to my eye.

Despite my moaning, though, I thought it wasn't that swollen. I mean, I could still see through it, which I figured had to be a good thing.

"You should probably stick some ice on that, or something," suggested Dec, looking at me uncertainly.

"Why? Is it really that obvious?" I said.

"Nonono," said Dec, quickly. "It's fine, nobody's going to notice, but maybe that'll help stop it from swelling up, or something."

OK, so that *sounded* reassuring, but from the way Dec was staring at me, I could tell something was wrong. And yep, either he was lying or there must have been some sort of delayed reaction, because by the time I got home. . . Well, let's just say my mum didn't take it anywhere near as calmly as I'd been expecting.

"Good day at school, Dylan?" she shouted from the kitchen. "Listen, I'm doing nutloaf for tea, and I don't want to hear any complaints because I've had a really tough *ohmygodwhathappenedtoyoureye*?"

"Cricket ball," I blurted out. To be honest, I hadn't even thought about what I was going to say, which was obviously a massive mistake.

"A *cricket ball*? What did your teachers say?"

"Well, nothing, really. I mean, it was an accident."

"Accident my. . . Do you *realize* what I'd have to deal with if I let someone in *my* class go home looking like you?"

"Yeah, but it was my fault really," I said, trying to stop Mum from ringing my school and *really* dropping me in it. "I went for a catch and sort of . . . let my face get in the way."

"I didn't realize it was cricket season,"

pointed out my sister Becky, strolling in from the kitchen. Typical Becky – even though she's enough of an airy-fairy hippy type to prefer nutloaf to (say) pepperoni pizza, she's logical enough to mess things up *just* when everything's going all right.

"Indoor cricket," I explained, thinking fast.

"With a proper cricket ball?" asked Becky, looking surprised.

"We're practising for the summer," I said, thinking even faster. "Anyway, I've got homework to do, so. . ."

"Honestly, look at it!" Mum carried on, grabbing my head for a better look. "Are you sure you haven't got concussion? What's our phone number?"

"I haven't got concussion, Mum," I insisted, desperately wanting to avoid having my head X-rayed.

"Maybe we should run you up to the hospital just in case. Becky, can you. . ."

"Nonono," said Becky. "I'm meeting someone tonight."

"Again?" I whipped my head round, which made it throb a bit. "Who's 'someone'?"

"He's called Charlie," said Becky – now *she*

was on the defensive, which made a nice change. "And it's none of your business."

"*He?*" I said. "Have you got a *date*, Becks?"

"We're just friends. . ." started Becky.

"Friends who snog?" I asked, not very helpfully. To be honest, I was quite pleased at the idea. Whoever this bloke was, he couldn't possibly be worse than Becky's last boyfriend – *Spider*, with his eleven piercings, vegan self-righteousness and annoying voice.

"Don't change the subject, Dylan," said Mum, still prodding at my head. She seemed to be calming down a bit. "Didn't they even give you an ice pack?"

"It happened right at the end of the day," I said. "And anyway, I thought you were supposed to put steak on black eyes."

"Euch. Just put some frozen peas on it," suggested Becky.

"We haven't got any peas, *or* any steak," said Mum, rummaging around in the freezer and eventually coming out with a bag. "You're going to have to make do with this."

"Mum," I said, looking at the packet in her hand. "I'm not holding a bag of frozen mince on my face. . ."

It Really Sets Off Your Eyes

"Are you wearing *make-up?*" asked Will, squinting at me.

"No," I said. "Don't be daft."

Well, that was a half-truth. "Make-up" sounds like I was plastered with mascara and lipstick, which I definitely *wasn't* – nothing draws attention to yourself on a boring Tuesday morning like turning up to school looking like Madonna, especially if you're a lad. The thing was, though, I'd been expecting my eye to go down a bit overnight, and it hadn't. If anything, it was *worse,* with splotches of purple and green that seemed to have *appeared* among the black overnight. When I looked at it in the bathroom mirror, I knew I couldn't just turn up at school with it – the teachers'd make the grilling I got off my mum look like a cosy chat. I was thinking of excuses when I spotted it. . . Mum's foundation. OK, so it wasn't *exactly* the same tone as my skin – more of a two-week suntan – but with a bit of experimental splodging and blending in, it sort of worked. If you saw it from a distance, and squinted a bit, you could hardly tell. Shame Will was sitting directly opposite me and staring at my face.

"Yes you are – your cheek's a different colour to the rest of your face," he insisted, prodding at it. "And your eye looks all puffy. What have you been up to?"

"Ow!" I yelped, batting his finger away from the sensitive bit of my face. "I got in a fight with the Lowfield kids, all right?"

OK, so "fight" might have been an exaggeration. But who wants to admit that they got punched in the face and let the other person totally get away with it?

"A *fight*?" said Will, looking as if I'd just told him I'd been attacked by space-chimps. "So you hit them back?"

"Well, yeah. . ." I started. Not strictly true, but even with Will – my wimpiest mate by far – it hurt to admit I'd just been on the receiving end of a one-punch beating. "I mean. . ."

"Well, I'd wash that orange gunk off, if I were you," advised Will. "If Matt sees you wearing make-up, you'll probably have to fight him as well."

"Who's been fighting?" came a girl's voice from behind me. "Oh, Dylan, what've you done to your *face*?"

I turned around. *Rachel.* No *way* was I going to fool her with a bit of tangerine-coloured splodge – she's practically got a GCSE in make-up.

"S'nothing," I mumbled. "Don't worry about it."

"You poor *thing*!" Rachel cooed, poking a long-nailed finger straight into my cheek. "Does it hurt?"

"Owww!" I yelped, momentarily forgetting my strong, silent image. "I mean, no, it's not that bad, as long as you don't touch it."

"You should see the Lowfield lads," interrupted Dec, helpfully, strolling up to our table and dumping his bag on it.

"Why, what happened to them?" asked Rachel, completely ignoring Dec and looking me in the eye.

"Erm. . ." I started, not sure where this was going.

Don't get me wrong – I'm always a big fan of sympathy from girls, but not when it comes with Idiots attached. And Idiots don't come much bigger than Matt Holland, an ex-mate of mine who turned to the dark side round about the time he got big enough to pick other kids up by their ankles. Rachel and Matt are like one of those couples you see in tatty gossip mags – totally loved-up one minute, then doing nothing but bitching about each other the next. What usually happens is, they hold hands and snog for a couple of weeks, then Matt does something stupid – like try to two-time Rachel with someone else. Then it's all sniffles and runny mascara and the It girls crowd round with tissues and scowl at Matt. Then there's a break – a week, usually, a fortnight at most – then Matt sends Keith, Nick, or one of his other deputy-Idiots to apologize and before you know it, they're at it again, making up for lost time with a retch-making marathon tongue-fest in the middle of the football pitch. Sometimes, Rachel falls for somebody else in the gap (like Andreas, Will's tree-sized German penfriend), but it's never long before they're back together. It's actually sort of sweet – in a really nauseating, horrible way. But anyway, the point is – flirting with Rachel's always going to be trouble. Big, scary, rugby-gorilla-attracting trouble. And I really wasn't sure if I could handle any more trouble in my life right at that second. On the other hand, I didn't *really* want to tell the truth, either – not with a rapidly expanding crowd of faces peering over Rachel's shoulders. "Someone punched me and wandered off" – how cool is *that*? But I didn't have a *clue* what to say instead. Fortunately, *somebody* did.

"Dylan mashed them," said Dec, breezily. "Three of them. It's just a shame one of them hit him from behind. But they'll know not to mess next time."

"Is that true, Dylan?" said Karen, one of Rachel's It girl mates, making big, moony, oh-you-poor-baby eyes at me. For just a second, I felt a lot better.

"Erm. . ." I said again, not sure whether to just give up.

"If they hit him from behind," added Hannah, "how come he's got a black eye on his *face*?"

"Did you really mash three Lowfield lads?" Chris shouted from a nearby table. Suddenly, I was the centre of attention.

"Well, *sort* of. . ." I said, reluctantly.

"Of *course* he did. . ." Dec said, slapping me on the back.

"I hope," came a stern voice from the front of the classroom, "that nobody from this class has been mashing anybody."

We looked round. Our form tutor, Mr Wallace, was standing, looking amused, in the doorway.

"Oh dear, Mr Douglas," he said, not looking very sympathetic. "What happened to your eye?"

"He. . ." started Rachel, only to be shushed by a hand from Mr Wallace.

"I believe I was addressing Mr Douglas," he said, calmly. "If I need an opinion from you, Rachel, I'll ask for it."

"I got thumped," I mumbled.

"Good lord," said Mr Wallace, raising an eyebrow but not really looking the slightest bit surprised. "And did you do any 'thumping' back?"

I lowered my voice another notch.

"Not really."

"Well, that's probably just as well," said Mr Wallace, shuffling in behind his desk. "Now – everyone in their seats. . ."

I took one last glance around and – sure enough – I was still getting stares. Most people just looked curious, a couple of them looked disapproving and one or two glances were what I suppose you'd call pitying. But the weirdest thing was, one or two people actually looked *impressed*. . .

"So. . ." said Kate, plonking herself down next to me with a tray full of fruit and pasta and other girl stuff. "What *really* happened to your eye?"

"Got in a fight," I mumbled, suddenly feeling very self-conscious about my own massive helping of soggy fries and rhubarb crumble.

"A *fight?*" said Kate.

"Yeah," I said. "Don't worry, I sorted them out."

"You did *what?*" Kate didn't look that impressed. In fact, she looked *horrified*.

"Well, not exactly," I admitted. "I mean, I might have hurt one bloke's knuckles. . ."

"Well. . ." said Kate, giving me an uncertain sort of smile. "I hope it's healed up by next Friday." She slid a bit of paper across the table. "I wouldn't want it interfering with your costume."

"What?" I said, remembering what Kate had said about Friday in the Virgin Megastore. Was she asking me out? Or. . . Then I looked at the bit of paper. "Oh. You're having a fancy dress party?"

I struggled to look excited, I really did.

"Mm-hm!" Kate nodded, smiling. "For my birthday! It's a Hollywood theme, so you can dress up as your favourite film character, or your favourite villain, or—"

"So who else is coming?" I interrupted, feeling slightly deflated.

"Well, everyone, really." Kate shrugged. "I didn't want to upset anyone, so I've given invitations to pretty much everybody in our year."

"Oh." Now I was *totally* depressed. Suddenly, my vision of being special and privileged had been replaced by one of me clamouring for Kate's attention over fifty other people.

". . .but, you know, I was really hoping you'd come," Kate carried on.

Whooooosh! Suddenly, my punctured ego rose up again like . . . well, a hot air balloon, or something. Yeah, so everyone was *invited,* but Kate *really wanted me to come.* Brilliant!

"So, um, what're you going as?" I asked, casually.

"Surprise," said Kate. "What about you? Any ideas?"

"Well, I dunno. . ." I said, "I mean, my favourite film's *Jaws*, but I can't exactly turn up as a massive shark. . ."

Kate punched me in the arm.

"Or I *could* go as Frodo from *Lord of the Rings*," I carried on, "I could just walk everywhere on my knees and wear a ring. It wouldn't be that difficult."

"You *could*, but everybody fancies Legolas," Kate pointed out. "Maybe you should get a white wig."

"Maybe," I said. "Look, can't you just give me a hint about what you're wearing? Just so I don't *totally* embarrass myself?"

"We-ell," said Kate. "I'm going to the costume shop on Thursday – you can come along, if you wan–"

"What happened to your eye, Dylan?" interrupted a voice behind me.

"Walked into a wall," I said, turning round. "And I'm getting sick of that question. What do you want?"

Standing next to our table was Matt "The Idiot" Holland and his motley crew of, well, Idiots. As I think I've mentioned, I used to be friends with Matt – way back when we both thought girls were weird and neither of us played rugby. Then one of us turned into a big, arrogant, Idiot. And then there was an incident with a fire extinguisher and another one with a very large German – but those are other stories. Let's just say, I wasn't expecting to get any sympathy from the Idiots. Which was why I was a bit surprised by what happened next.

"No, seriously, mate," said Matt. "We want to know."

There was a general shuffling and nodding of heads behind him. This was weird. I'd have expected the Idiots to be laughing their heads off at me getting thumped – instead, they actually seemed *concerned.* And Matt had called me "mate" for the first time in, well, as long as I could remember? This was *seriously* weird.

"I, erm, it was, um. . ." I started, not sure whether to – ahem – *expand* on the truth. I knew that if Dec was telling the story he'd have been injured single-handedly fighting off an entire *class* of ginger psychos. In the end, though, I decided to go for the truth. "I got thumped by some kid from Lowfield."

Matt glowered.

"I bloody knew it. . ." he said, nodding slowly. "Lowfield scum."

"Don't worry, Dylan," added Keith, nodding, as Kate gave him a dirty look. "We'll sort them out."

There were a lot more nods and murmurs, and I think – I *think* – I heard someone cracking their knuckles at the back. Hmm.

"So, you want us to walk you home tonight?" said Matt, putting on his best rugby-player face.

"What? No!" I blurted, a bit ashamed to be getting this sort of babysitting treatment in front of Kate, who didn't look even *remotely* impressed by all the macho posing going on. "No, I'll be fine, thanks. If there's any trouble, I'll sort it out."

OK, so I wasn't *sure* that was true, but there was something about the way Matt was acting that was making me nervous. I mean, was he *really* concerned about me – or was he just looking at me as an excuse for a fight?

It's Good to Stalk

"My mum says you're supposed to stand up to bullies," said Will, glancing nervously behind him.

"Your mum," said Dec, not looking reassured, "went to school in the 1960s. Bullies were different back then – if you stand up to them these days, they kick your head in."

"My mum's not *that* old," huffed Will, defensively.

OK, so I'd seemed brave when I was talking to Matt, but my confidence was fading on the long walk home. Still, even with my two mates bickering like this, it felt good having them on either side of me. I wasn't kidding myself that Will would have a chance against Grunty, but at least there were three of us, which might put the Lowfield posse off a bit. Also, we'd changed our normal route home into a massive Lowfield-avoiding crescent, so I reckoned that the chances of us accidentally running into trouble were pretty slim. Still, that wasn't stopping Dec from checking out every street like a Navy SEAL on heavy reconnaissance, peering out from behind bushes and walls until he was sure the coast was clear.

"Why are *you* so worried, anyway?" I asked, while Dec was scoping out a particularly dodgy-looking car wash for ginger activity. "*I'm* the one who got punched."

"Yeah, but they might have gone for the wrong person."

"What d'you mean?" I asked, looking at Dec.

"Well, they could've been after someone from our school," said Dec, nervously. "Anyone, I mean – and they saw your uniform, and they thought. . ."

Der-der-der-der-der-der! went Dec's phone. I almost jumped into a tree.

Dec, who looked like he'd almost been ready to cling on to *Will*, got his cool back in record time, stared at the screen, gave a dismissive little snort and ignored it.

"Was that the stalker?" I said.

"Yep."

"Maybe you should just send her a text," I suggested. "Y'know, just to let her know you're not interested."

"Yeah, but I don't want to encourage her," said Dec. "She's a complete bunny boiler."

"Well, that shouldn't be a problem for you," pointed out Will. "I mean, you haven't even got a bunny. . ."

"Shut up, Will," said Dec, then carried on, "I mean, it's not as if I can see her again anyway. . ."

"Why not?"

"Because. . . Ah, look, I just can't, all right?"

"*Where* did you say this girl's from again?" I asked, suddenly suspicious about this girl I'd never seen.

"Well," said Dec, looking edgier than ever, "I met her at the skatepa—"

"*Ginger!*" shouted Will, using the same sort of tone you'd normally save for yelling "shark!" at a beach.

"Where?" squeaked Dec, looking like he was ready to dive under a bush. Then we spotted the person Will was pointing at, and relaxed.

"That isn't him, Will," Dec said, giving the terrified-looking eleven-year-old ginger kid across the street a friendly wave. The kid waved back nervously, but he still looked as if he was half-thinking about making a run for it. I didn't really blame him – the sight of a gang of older kids pointing at you and shouting doesn't do your nerves any good at all.

"For future reference, Will," said Dec, "the lad we're scared of is *bigger* than us."

"Sorry," mumbled Will. "How was I supposed to know?"

"*Anyway,*" Dec said firmly, ignoring Will and turning to me. "How's it going with Kate?"

"It isn't, really," I said, a bit glumly. "I mean, there's the party on Friday, but *everyone's* invited to that."

"Hey, the party!" said Dec, brightening up. Of *course* Kate had invited him – she'd practically carpet-bombed our class with invitations, so even *Will* had managed to get one. "That's your chance! You can go as . . . as a bear, or something."

"A *bear?*" I said, incredulously. Honestly, sometimes I think I've worked out how Dec's mind works, and then he says something that *totally* throws me off again.

"Or *something,*" said Dec, looking offended.

"Girls like bears. Look, you've got to do *something.* She's going to be all dressed up at this party, and all the lads are going to be going for her, and you're going to be standing in the corner dressed as a clown or whatever, and in a couple of weeks you'll be her mate who she talks to about how annoying her boyfriend is."

"Wow." I said. That was quite a mental image. And it was about the worst thing that could happen – I'd have to pretend not to be bothered while she was wandering around with someone else, holding hands and sno. . . I decided to stop thinking about that possibility.

"Maybe you should just give up on her," Dec carried on, taking his usual sensitive tack. "Haven't you noticed how interested in you the *rest* of the girls are?"

"They were poking me in the eye, Dec," I insisted, reflexively prodding at my face and wincing. "I don't think that counts."

"Sure it does. They were all over you. You've got to be more *aggressive*, Dylan," insisted Dec. "Girls *love* that stuff. Didn't you see the way Rachel and Karen looked at you when they found out you'd beaten up the Lowfield lads?"

"When you *told* them that's what I did," I corrected.

"Whatever," Dec carried on. "The main thing is, girls like lads who can take care of themselves. Haven't you noticed how popular Matt is?"

"Yeah, but I *can't* take care of myself," I pointed out, feeling miserable. "Matt would've probably rugby-tackled them to the floor, or something, but I just got thumped."

"Don't be so down on yourself," insisted Dec. "They took you by surprise, remember? And anyway, I've got an idea. . ."

I looked down and read the yellow flyer.

Learn Aiki-Jitsu!
Meet New People!
Gain Self-Confidence!
Get Fit!

Underneath, there was a load of stuff about how the teacher – sorry, *sensei* – was a sixth dan (whatever that means) trained by, erm, somebody-or-other, and how Aiki-Jitsu was an ancient and traditional martial art. It all sounded very professional and everything – despite the dodgy photocopying – but somehow, I wasn't convinced. I mean, did *real* kung-fu masters advertise their classes in the window of the local Post Office?

"Great, eh?" said Dec. "I *knew* I'd seen that flyer before. It's on tomorrow. And Friday."

"Meet new people?" I asked, raising an eyebrow. Well, I would have raised an eyebrow, but I can't. I've spent hours in the bathroom practising, but. . . Well, anyway.

"And beat them up!" Dec said, excitedly. "Sounds brilliant, doesn't it?"

"I'm not sure," was all I could come up with. However much self-confidence I had, I didn't think it was going to discourage nutters from smacking me in the face. As for getting fit – well, at least I'd be able to run away properly. "I mean, I don't think the way to avoid getting punched's going to a martial arts lesson where *everybody's trying to hit you,*" I said.

"Don't worry, mate," said Dec, looking nonchalant. "It's like skateboarders say – bruises heal, and girls love scars."

"What are you on about?" I said. "You haven't got any scars."

"Yes I have," Dec insisted, rolling up his sleeve to show off a patch of elbow that was *slightly* more pink than the rest. "What d'you call that?"

"A graze," I said. "And you didn't even get that skateboarding – that's from tripping over a hose."

This was true. Dec had told the story before – he'd been having a water-fight with some cousin or other in his back garden when he was eight, then he managed to get his feet tangled up in a garden hose and skinned his elbow on the gravel driveway. Screamed for hours, according to his mum.

"Yeah?" said Dec. "Well, let's see yours."

Sigh. The truth is, I haven't got any cool scars. There's a little one on my chin (mountain bike crash), one on my finger (origin unknown), and a tiny one on my forehead (can of rice pudding falling out of a cupboard when I opened it). It's sort of embarrassing.

"So what d'you reckon?" Dec said, interrupting my thoughts by waving the flyer uncomfortably close to my face. I thought about Gary Pierce, Matt the Idiot and – very briefly – Jean-Claude Van Damme.

"Nope," I said. "No way. I mean, we haven't even had any hassle today, have we?"

Yeah, went my brain. *All you have to do is walk an extra two miles home every day and you'll be fine.*

Which didn't exactly make me feel better. . .

That's How Houdini Died, Y'Know

"Hwuff!"

Not too bad, I thought. *Let's try that a bit harder.*

"Hwuff!"

And again.

"HWUFF!"

OK, so to anyone watching, the sight of me standing in the living room punching myself in the stomach in front of the Tuesday evening repeat of *The Weakest Link* might have seemed a *bit* weird – I mean, I know everyone hates Anne Robinson, but it's not *that* bad. But with nobody in my house, it seemed like the perfect time to try getting a bit of exercise in. After all, the *last* thing I wanted to do was spray Doritos and bits of carrot across the room if I got hit in the stomach, even if I was refusing to have anything to do with

Dec's insane kung-fu fantasies. After doing as many sit-ups as I could (nineteen, although the last three were a bit shaky) there was still no sign of an emerging six-pack, but it definitely seemed a *bit* firmer. Of course, that might have just been my stomach muscles locking up in protest at the first exercise they'd ever been forced to do. Now – press-ups.

I made it to sixteen before my arms started wobbling.

"Hwuff!"

I could feel myself going red in the face.

"Hweurgh!"

No pain, no gain, went one bit of my brain.

"Hrrrr!"

You're going to pop a blood vessel in your head, went another.

"Hweeergh!"

Come on! went my brain. I pictured Jean-Claude having coconuts dropped on his stomach and kicking palm trees.

"Hwwwrrrffff!"

I collapsed. Brilliant.

"What," said a voice from the doorway, "are you *doing?"*

"Waargh!" was the first thing I said, closely

followed by a slightly more casual, "What? Oh, just watching a bit of telly."

Yeah, right. Because I often watch TV lying on the floor and sweating. *So* much better than relaxing on the sofa. I propped myself on my elbows and looked round.

Aaaargh.

Becky would have been bad. And yeah, of course it was her, giving me an evil little smirk – but worse, so was one of her crazy hippy mates. There was something weird about this one, though. I couldn't work it out. Same floppy, falling-to-bits jumper, same messy, tied-back hair, same ridiculous clumpy boots. . . And then I worked it out. It was a *bloke.*

Still, I thought. *No piercings. That has to be a good sign.*

"You must be Dylan," said the mystery bloke. "I'm Charlie."

Charlie. The mystery bloke from the other night. He shook my hand, which was a bit embarrassing, considering the sweaty state of my palms – but he didn't seem to mind. I must have looked surprised, though, because Becky was pulling a "Don't-you-dare" face at me behind Charlie's back.

"Um, nice to meet you," I said, in my best meeting-people voice.

"What happened to your eye?"

"Cricket ball," I said, out of reflex more than anything else.

"Wow," said Charlie. "You should be, y'know, *careful* when you're playing cricket."

"Yeah," I said, still a bit embarrassed.

"And careful when you're watching TV as well," Charlie added, although he was smiling instead of doing the sneer I'd have expected from Spider. "You don't want to give yourself a hernia."

My sister practically exploded in giggles.

Typical, I thought. *Just when I was starting to like him. . .*

Just then, the front door slammed again.

"Hi, Mum," chorused Becky and me.

"Hi," came the subdued-sounding reply. Then, Mum walked in. And you know that expression, "having the world on your shoulders"? Well, for the first time I could really see what that looked like – she was sort of *drooping* in a way that just didn't look like my usual, bright 'n' bouncy mum. Of course, that might have been something to do with the two huge carrier bags full of assorted folders and books she was carrying.

"Um, did you have a good day at school?" tried Becky.

"Not really," said Mum, slumping into a chair.

"I'll put the kettle on, shall I?" offered Charlie, strolling off into the kitchen without waiting for an answer. Yep, he was *definitely* a lot more friendly than Spider.

"Who's *that*?" whispered Mum. "He's very polite, isn't he?"

"That's Becky's *boyfriend*," I said. Oh, come on – you've got to play the "annoying little brother" card sometimes.

"He's not my. . . He's just a. . . Oh, never mind. . ." said Becky, flushing bright red. It looked like I wasn't the *only* person who was having problems in the friend zone. . .

Surely That's a Foul, Ref?

However worried I was about the friendship circle, though, there were other, more black-eye related things to take my mind off it. Like: could I *really* cope with dodging Matt's vigilante posse, followed by an extra-long walk home every day for the rest of my school life? Yeah, the extra distance was probably keeping me fit, but it wasn't exactly stress-free. By Wednesday evening, I was already a nervous wreck. And no, watching two men in tights cuddle each other wasn't *exactly* how I'd pictured relaxing that evening.

"Ooooh!" chorused Will and Dec.

It's a funny thing, but my two best mates don't really get on that well. I mean, they hang around with each other and everything, but I sometimes get the feeling that they're only doing it for my benefit – that if I was suddenly forced to flee the country (or whatever) they'd never speak to each other again. Except for when they're watching wrestling.

"Ohhhh!" they shouted, in perfect unison, watching Wrestler A (long, sweaty hair, tanned and muscular, tights) smash Wrestler B (no hair at all, a bit flabby, tights) over the head with a chair. This is the other great thing about Dec's house – he's got some kind of cable TV set-up that gets *every channel in the world*. Whatever you want to do – buy an ornamental cuckoo clock off the auction channel or watch the men's qualifiers of Burmese Volleyball – chances are you'll be able to see it at Dec's house. As long as his mum isn't in.

"Ooooh!" they shouted again, as Wrestler B kicked out of a pin at the last possible second.

"So," I tried to interrupt. "Any ideas about this fancy dress party?"

"No," said Will and Dec together. Wrestler A was hoisting Wrestler B up on to the turnbuckle to try some sort of finishing move – although from where I was sitting, it looked an awful lot like Wrestler B was climbing.

"I was thinking about something that covers up my eye. . ." I carried on.

"A clown," said Dec, not looking away from the TV.

"A vampire," said Will.

"Or a boxer," said Dec.

Hmm. I had to admit, that sounded OK. But then I thought about what boxers traditionally wear – I mean, it's a vest and shorts at most – and *then* I thought about my weedy, sixteen-press-up arms. I decided against it.

"What're *you* two going as?"

"Dunno," said Dec, finally glancing over at me. "Maybe a skateboarder."

"You *are* a skateboarder," I said, not really surprised by the laziness of this plan. "And anyway, it's supposed to be *Hollywood* themed. How many films have you seen about skateboarders?"

"Mmm," said Dec, turning back to the TV. "Y'know, maybe you could pick up some fighting tips off these wrestlers."

"It's not real, Dec," I pointed out. "Y'know, like the tooth fairy."

"The tooth fairy's not real?" Dec gave me a mock-surprised look. "So who keeps giving me those fifty pees?"

"Anyway, it still hurts," interrupted Will, pointing to another wrestler, currently getting a chair kicked in his face. I had to admit, it looked pretty painful. "You can't fake that stuff."

"So I'm supposed to start carrying a chair around?"

"Maybe one of the Year Elevens do that for you," said Dec. "Another one of them asked me what the guys in the Lowfield posse looked like today. . ."

"Hey!" said Will, suddenly struck by inspiration. "You could go dressed as that guy!" He pointed out a tiny wrestler wearing a mask, currently leaping off the turnbuckle to flatten someone twice his size. "That'd cover your eye!"

"Will," I said. "He's not in a film. And anyway, where am I going to get a mask like that?"

"Oh yeah. . ." Will trailed off, looking disappointed.

"Wait a sec," said Dec, levering himself up. "I've got an idea."

He dashed out of the room, leaving me and Will to watch the wrestlers.

"So, y'know, what *will* you do if you see the Lowfield posse again?" asked Will. Good old Will – Dec can put up a brave front, but seeing my other best mate in a panic always makes me feel a bit better.

"Dunno," I said. "Probably run for it."

"Yeah, but you can't do that for ever, can you?" said Will. "And I can't run that fast."

"Will," I said. "They're not even after you."

"Yeah, but why're they picking on *you*?" Will said. "I mean, we haven't done anything to. . ."

Der-der-der-der-der-der!

Dec's phone started dancing across the table as it flashed and vibrated where he'd left it. I sneaked a quick look at the display as it buzzed itself closer and closer to the edge of his mum's hideous coffee table.

"Erika P?" I said, looking at Will.

He shook his head.

"Never heard of her."

Then we both thought of the same thing.

"Stalker!" I hissed.

"Answer it!" Will hissed back.

"You answer it!"

"*I* can't answer it, Dec'll kill me!"

"Well, *I* can't answer it, he'll. . . Oh, never mind."

I snatched the still-buzzing phone off the table, flipped open the lid and hit Answer. "Um, hello?"

"Hiiiieee!" came a loud enough squeal to make me pull the phone away from my ear quickly. "Where have you been? I've been trying to get through to you for *days*. But anyway, that doesn't matter, because now I can tell you about–"

"Errrr," I said, trying to interrupt before she started telling me she loved me, "this isn't *actually* Dec."

"Oh." There was a pause on the other end of the line, then a slightly more deflated-sounding Erica P carried on. "So how come you're answering his phone?"

"Because he's gone to get a pair of tights or something," I nearly said, then settled for, "He's, um, busy."

"Oh," said a slightly grumpier sounding Erika. "Well, how long's he going to be busy for?"

I glanced up. Dec had reappeared in the doorway, wearing – and I don't know quite how to put this – a sock with a face scribbled on it on one hand. I didn't know exactly what to say – apart from, maybe, "Sorry, Dec's just gone totally insane."

Stalker, I mouthed at him.

Hang up, he mouthed back.

"Hello?" came Erika's voice from the other end of the phone.

"Sorry, I've got to um, go. . ."

I passed the phone to Dec, and he jabbed the End Call button without saying a word.

"Hey, nice idea!" said Will. "Mr *Socko,*" he explained to me, "he's, like a wrestler's prop."

"She seemed, um, nice. . ." I tried, ignoring Will.

"She's a nutcase," Dec assured me.

"Dec," I said. "You're the one with a sock on your hand."

Fighting Like a Girl

As it turned out, I might as well have taken Will's advice. If I'd worn a mask to school *every day*, I'd still have been less conspicuous than I was with my now-fading eye. Everywhere I went, somebody seemed to be pointing me out – whether it was giggly Year Sevens or too-cool Year Elevens. By Thursday, I'd expected things to calm down, but they seemed worse than ever. And *some* people seemed to be taking my safety *far* too seriously.

"Matt's looking for you," Dec said, casually, strolling up to me near the end of the day.

"What? Why?" I really didn't like this. You know how in some Bugs Bunny cartoons there's that huge monster that always wants to hug him but nearly ends up crushing him to death? That's a bit like how I felt about being friends with Matt.

"I think he's forming some sort of vigilante squad," Dec said, cheerfully. "He's been talking to all the hard lads from the other years, and I think they're getting ready for some sort of massive scrap."

"Who is?" said Kate, strolling up.

"Erm. . ." said Dec.

"It's nothing," I said, quickly. "Apparently Matt wants to walk me home."

"Nope, *I'm* walking you home," said Kate, turning to me. "We're going to the costume shop, remember?"

Dec gave me a quick thumbs-up and a massive grin, then disappeared off down the corridor. And left me to one of the worst evenings of my life.

I've talked to girls before, and mostly, I'm rubbish at it. If I fancy them, I'm so worried about what they're going to think that I can hardly string a sentence together, let alone come up with something funny to say. But it wasn't like that with Kate – I could just *talk* to her. *Yeah,* said my brain, occasionally. *Because you're in the friend zone. She doesn't actually fancy you at all.* It was probably because I was in the middle of thinking something like that that I didn't notice the little group coming the other way up the road. In fact, I would have probably walked straight past them, if one of them hadn't intentionally shoulder-barged into me.

"Look who it is!" said Pizza Boy, looking almost pleased to see me. "How's the eye?"

"Fine," I growled. Well, I *say* growled, because that's what I *meant* to do. It actually came out as more of a whimper.

"Come back for more, have you?" Pizza Boy carried on, still looking quite happy.

What I should have said, obviously, is something like: "No, of course not. I've got no interest in fighting. I don't think it's big, hard or clever, and I'm actually a pacifist." Then I could've sung a quick verse of "Give Peace a Chance", and they might have left me alone.

But because Kate was there, and I thought I still had the *tiniest* chance of clinging to the myth of my kung-fu superpowers, what I *actually* said was:

"I'm warning you, mate – leave it."

"Oooo-oooh!" sang Pizza Boy. "'Leave it.' I'm scared now."

"Hurrr," went Grunty.

"Hey!" interrupted Kate, stepping in front of me. "Leave him alone. He hasn't done anything to you."

Ah. It looked like Kate didn't exactly believe the bit about me beating the three of them up, anyway.

"Oooh!" sneered Pizza Boy again, as if he'd only just noticed her. "Brought your *girlfriend* to look after you, have you?"

"Actually. . ." I started.

"It doesn't *matter* who I am," Kate said, ignoring me. "Just leave us alone."

Under other circumstances, I'd have liked to stop there and say something like: "Well, actually, Kate, it does matter, quite a lot. I mean, I'd *like* you to be my girlfriend, and I'm quite pleased that these lads assumed that's what you are. Even if they are a bunch of psychos." But I didn't get a chance, because that was when GP decided to speak.

"Where's your mate?"

"He's, um. . ." I started, a bit confused by the new line of questioning, but at that moment, Kate decided to take advantage of the pause in hostilities to make her move.

"Come on, Dylan," she said, grabbing my hand and half-leading, half-dragging me across the road.

Again, under other circumstances, this would've been great. I mean, not only was I holding hands with Kate, but she obviously liked me enough to risk saving me from a gang of bullies.

Unfortunately, I couldn't really enjoy the moment, because:

a) My palms were a bit sweaty from all the excitement, and I couldn't help worrying about whether Kate thought I was always this clammy.

b) Kate had saved me from a beating. I thought this *had* to damage my credibility, somehow. And, most importantly. . .

c) Pizza Boy picked that moment to shout: "TART!" across the road.

I should probably have said something, right? I mean, if I've learned anything from Jean-Claude Van Damme films it's that you're not supposed to let gangs of bad guys call your (potential) girlfriend a tart. But I only got as far as turning round and saying, "You. . ." before Kate tugged on my (sweaty) hand and hissed, "Come *on*." Neither of us looked back, and before I knew it, we were round the corner and out of insult range, without any footsteps behind us.

"Thanks," was the first thing I said to Kate – followed by, slightly more stupidly, "but you didn't have to do that. I could've had them, you know."

"Right," said Kate, breaking hand-contact now that the danger was over.

"No, but I *could* have," I insisted.

"It doesn't matter, though, does it, Dylan?" said Kate, looking straight at me. "I mean, there's nothing big about fighting."

"Yeah," I said, suddenly ashamed of myself. "I know. But I *could* have. . ."

"But you didn't have to."

"Yeah," I sulked. "But. . . Look, I'm just going to go home, OK?"

"OK," said Kate, firmly. "See you tomorrow."

Nice one, Dylan, went my brain. When we'd started walking home, I'd thought that I had a chance – yeah, an outside chance, but still a chance – of getting a snog. Now even a peck on the cheek seemed out of the question.

"Bye," I said, and trudged off. *Think of something clever,* suggested my brain. *You don't have to leave it like this.*

Great, went my brain, and shut itself down. At the end of school, I'd had an hour of flirting and trying on costumes to look forward to, an annoyed Matt to gloat about and Kate chatting to me. Now I didn't even have an *outfit.*

Ten minutes later, I finally made it home, shrugged off my schoolbag and immediately phoned Dec.

"Heyyy!" he practically shouted down the phone. "How did it go? What did you. . ." He suddenly lowered his voice to a half-serious whisper. "She isn't still with you, is she?"

"Shut up, Dec," I interrupted. "I think we should go to the kung-fu lessons."

The Ancient Art of Punching Stuff

"So what's this thing you're going to tonight, Dylan?" asked my mum. "Judo?"

Friday at school had crawled by. Apart from avoiding eye contact with Matt's entire gang and more questions from Year Seven about the Lowfield lads, there was German to do, maths homework I'd forgotten about, and Dec pestering me about the *exact* details of what happened with Kate and the Lowfield posse.

Now I was back at home eating another of my sister's brilliant culinary creations – mushroom casserole, she explained with a little sniff – and I wasn't entirely sure if I was going to have the energy to do *anything*. Not unless I grabbed some chocolate on the way to the sports centre.

"Aiki-jitsu," I corrected. "It's a form of self-defence that uses an attacker's own strength against him."

OK, so that was a direct quote from the flyer Dec had given me, but you have to admit it sounded good.

"Sounds dangerous," said my mum, uncertainly.

"Sounds *stupid,*" added Becky, showing her usual level of encouragement. "You should learn something constructive, like tai chi."

"Becky," interrupted my dad, "is there garlic in this?"

"Yep," said my sister, looking pleased with herself.

"Did you, um, cook it or anything?"

"No. . ." said Becky, looking a bit unsure of herself. "Why?"

"No reason," said Dad, looking as if he was having trouble swallowing.

"Are you going to be using weapons?" persisted Mum, still looking a bit anxious.

"Nope," I said. Secretly, I was sort of hoping we would, but I didn't think this was an outright lie. I mean, they probably wouldn't let us near the swords until we'd been training for at least, ooh, a couple of weeks. I munched an under-cooked mushroom. "No accessories needed. That's why it's called 'the way of the empty hand'. . ."

"Will." Dec frowned. "Why're you carrying a badminton racket?"

Of course, Will was terrified about asking his mum's permission to go to Aiki-jitsu. That's why I'd come up with the brilliant idea of, erm, not bothering. After all, the badminton court was at the sports centre – so was Aiki-jitsu. Badminton kept you fit – so did Aiki-jitsu. Aiki-jitsu was all about learning to hit people – badminton was all about learning to hit, erm, shuttlecocks. Even if Will's mum *did* find out what he was really up to, I reckoned he could probably just pretend he'd got confused and wandered into the wrong room. Will, of course, didn't exactly see it that way. And, even once we'd explained what was happening to Dec, he wasn't exactly encouraging.

"What if you get smacked in the face?" he asked, seeming quite cheerful about the idea. "How're you going to explain that?"

"That's not going to happen . . . is it?" Will asked, nervously.

"Of course not," I said, feeling less confident than I sounded. "It's all about learning to use the other person's strength against them and stuff. Nobody's going to get punched in the face."

Twenty minutes later, I wasn't feeling so sure.

"Kiai!" shouted a very red-faced man in white pyjamas and a brown belt.

"GYAAAH!" shouted the other twenty people running around the room.

By the time we got to the lesson, we were obviously late. It was partly because we'd had trouble finding the right room at the back of the huge sports centre, and partly because of a quick argument in the changing room about whether we should go in with our shoes on or off . . . and whether Will should go in brandishing his badminton racket. Anyway, when we finally made it into the dojo, it looked like they'd started without us.

A couple of dozen people – fat and thin, tall and short, beardy and completely bald, but mostly a lot older than us – were huffing and puffing their way around a room about half the size of our school canteen, bare feet slapping on the rubber mats covering the floor. A couple of them were wearing tracksuit bottoms and

T-shirts, like me, Will and Dec, but most were in proper traditional karate uniforms, sort of off-white and heavy-looking. None of them were talking. None of them were smiling. Most of them were sweating a lot. It almost reminded me of one of our PE sessions.

The only person not running had to be Sensei Moody himself. Short, wide and serious-looking, he had that special sort of skinhead haircut that some people get to disguise the fact that they're going bald. You know, that "No, I've *decided* to look like this" bluff that's scuppered as soon as you notice how shiny the front of their head is. As cover-ups go, it's about one step below a Homer Simpson comb-over. He was pacing up and down in the middle of the room in a special extra-wide black trouser/skirt combo, and looking even more serious than everyone else.

"We could just run away now," whispered Will.

"Yeah, I'm not sure this was a good idea," I hissed back.

"It'll be fine. . ." said Dec, calmly sauntering on to the mat.

"You!" the teacher said, spinning around to look straight at him. "Drop and give me twenty."

"Twenty what?" asked Dec, looking confused.

"Press-ups," said the teacher. Dec hesitated. "NOW!"

Dec looked around as if he was expecting someone to explain what was happening, then got down on his knees on a bit of mat where it looked like he wouldn't get trampled and started doing half-hearted press-ups. The teacher turned back to us.

"You two," he said, putting his hands by his sides and doing a little bow towards Will and me. "Make sure your friend knows – you *always* bow when you come on to the mat. Now, get running."

A lot of running, lots of star jumps and far too many sit-ups later, the teacher finally gave the order to line up, and everyone ran to the edge of the mat. After a bit of shuffling, we realized we were supposed to be in order, with the different grades lining up next to each other, the white belts last and anybody wearing tracksuits (which was us) squeezed in on the end. Finally, the teacher spoke: "Evening, everyone."

"Evening, SENSEI," bellowed the most enthusiastic people – most of whom seemed to be up at the other end of the class. I was starting to think being a black belt was all about being able to shout the loudest.

"I see we've got a couple of new people around tonight. Now, in a minute we're going to pair up and. . . Would you mind sitting in seiza like everyone else, please?"

There was a pause while everyone looked down the line to see who he was talking to. All the people in uniforms had knelt down and put their hands on their knees – I'd copied them, and so had Will. Dec was sitting with his legs straight in front of him, leaning backwards and staring at a spot on the ceiling. Slowly, he realized that everyone was staring at him.

"Sorry," he mumbled, shuffling into the proper kneeling position.

"Sorry *sensei*," added Moody.

"Oh, you don't have to apologize," said Dec.

"Twenty press-ups," Moody said, looking like he was struggling to stay in peaceful Zen sensei mode. "Now, if we can just. . ."

Der-der-derrrr! came a sudden, familiar buzz from the corner where we'd dumped our bags.

"Whose. Phone. Is that?" said Moody, through clenched teeth.

Like a flash, Dec abandoned his half-hearted

press-ups and dashed over to grab his phone – then took one look at the screen, shook his head in disgust and stuck it back in his bag. And then he noticed everyone staring at him. Again.

"Sorry about that," he said, shrugging, then mouthed *stalker* at me.

"No mobile phones in the dojo," Moody was starting to look seriously ready to demonstrate some techniques on Dec. "Down and give me. . ."

"Yeah, yeah, ten press-ups," said Dec, dropping on to his knees with a groan.

"*Fifty*," said Moody. "Everyone else find a partner. . ."

The first technique we learnt was a wristlock. There wasn't any punching or kicking involved – in fact, the move started from an innocent-looking handshake. The idea was to twist your grip around so you were pinning the other person's hand against your forearm, then use your other hand to lever down in their wrist. If you did it hard enough, as Moody demonstrated, they'd drop to the floor, so you could choose whether to walk away or knee them in the face. Or that was the idea, anyway.

"This is stupid. . . Is that hurting?" Dec asked, twisting my wrist like a difficult-to-open jam jar.

I shook my head – apart from giving me a bit of a Chinese burn, it wasn't having any effect at all. "I mean, how're you supposed to get them to shake hands. . . How about now?" I shook my head again. "And it's not like you can say to a mugger, OK, just hold my hand while I do *this*. . . Look, isn't that hurting at *all*?"

"You're doing it wrong," I said, shifting my grip around. "I think you do it like . . . *this*."

"Aaaah!" yelled Dec, followed by a word that definitely wasn't appropriate for a peaceful Zen master.

"No swearing in the dojo," said Moody, strolling past. "Ten press-ups."

"But he was breaking my wrist!" Dec protested. "And it's not really a dojo. . ."

"On your knuckles," said Moody, leaning in towards me on his way past. "Nice technique."

Will, meanwhile, was partnered up with one of the big yellow belts, and seemed to be picking everything up at lightning speed. When I glanced over, the concentration on his face made it look like he was tackling a tricky physics problem instead of just fighting someone: weight *here* plus a twist *here* equals the other person *slamming into the mat*. He glanced over and gave me a little thumbs up as the yellow belt picked himself up for the twentieth time.

But we weren't finished there – oh no. There were lots more clever ways of hurting people to go, including several more wristlocks, all of them getting increasingly complex and increasing the chances that you'd have to stop halfway through and try to work out which way the other person's hand was supposed to go. Which I didn't think would be too handy in a fight. Nope, for all-out fighting skills, my favourite move had to be the mastoid pinch. It turns out that you've got this little set of muscles at either side of your jaw – your mastoids – that don't seem to exist for any reason except to *really hurt* when someone squeezes them. It hurts so much, in fact, that if someone's strangling you (for instance), it'll practically *force* them to let go – unless they're really fat and you can't find their mastoids under all their chins, obviously.

Anyway, by five to eight, we were all completely knackered, aching all over and sick of being prodded in the throat. And Sensei Moody *still* wasn't finished.

"Right then! Line up! Horse stance! Twenty punches! And kiai after every punch."

"Kiai?" I whispered.

"He means shout," whispered back one of the blue belts.

"Quiet!" shouted Sensei Moody. "Horse stance! Ichi!"

Everyone threw punches, and a few of the brown belts let out explosive little shouts of "Ha!"

Down at our end, nobody made a sound. Moody didn't look impressed.

"I said *shout*! ICHI!"

"HA!" shouted a few more people.

"Ni!"

"HAA!" everyone joined in.

"San!"

"HAAA!"

"Shi!"

"HAAAAA!!"

"Ya-me!"

"HAAAA!" me, Dec and Will shouted.

"Actually, that means 'finish'," whispered a brown belt.

"Oh."

"My throat hurts," grumbled Will, still clutching his badminton racket as we dragged ourselves home.

"Yeah, well, my throat *and* my wrist *and* my arms hurt," moaned Dec. "He's a complete sadist. What're we supposed to do, anyway, shout bullies to death?"

"I think it's all about focusing your mind," I said, trying to remember if any of Lennon's kung-fu films involved scenes of mind-focusing screaming. Strangely, I couldn't remember any – and most of them had involved some sort of unconventional exercise routine, like fighting blindfolded or beating up giant straw dummies or getting your legs tied to trees, or something. How come we hadn't done any of that?

"And he kept making me do press-ups," moaned Dec. Poor old Dec. He's so used to getting his own way at home that being forced to bow and be all respectful's a complete shock for him. Will, on the other hand, seemed to have got used to it really quickly – although I wasn't entirely surprised. After all, Sensei Moody wasn't anywhere near as scary as Will's mum. I had to admit, though, my arms were really starting to stiffen up. All I wanted to do right now was have a big, steaming-hot bath, then spend the entire weekend lying in bed and watching telly.

"See you later," I mumbled to Dec and Will, after walking as far as we could huddled together for protection. On the rest of the way home, I tried to project don't-mess-with-me vibes, but since the only person I passed was an old man with a tiny yappy dog, I'm not sure if it worked or not.

"Have you packed yet?" said my dad as I got in. "We're leaving for Lennon's first thing in the morning, remember?"

Anyone for Tea?

"Is everything OK at school, Dylan?" asked my mum, in her worst trying-to-be-casual voice.

I've got to admit, she's got good timing.

At home, I'd have heard that warning tone straight away, mumbled something about homework and scooted upstairs to the safety of my own turf. But here I was, trapped in a car speeding along the motorway, fifteen miles from the nearest service station with a slowly fading black eye and a quickly reddening face. Don't get me wrong – I'd *tried* to get out of going. I'd promised to stay in the house, behave myself, even listen to Becky and eat her weird idea of vegetarian sausages if it meant avoiding two hours in a car with my parents. None of it did any good: my parents obviously thought I'd go out looking for fights as soon as they pulled out of the drive – and anyway, they'd decided that the car would be the ideal spot for an impromptu interrogation. I tried to sound casual.

"Yeah." Not good. That came out much higher than I expected – more like a squeak than the dismissive grunt I was going for. I tried harder on the next word. "Why?"

"I think it's fairly obvious, Dylan," said Mum, turning around to look at me. "You come home with a black eye, then you announce that you're taking up judo. . ."

"Aiki-jitsu," I said, then wished I'd kept my mouth shut.

"Look," said my mum, "if you're being bullied, you can *tell* us."

Honestly. Parents, eh? They go on about all that best-days-of-your-life stuff, and they obviously don't remember what it's like being at school at all. I mean, I could be wrong, but I'm pretty sure that if you get a job in a bank you don't have to worry about people from other banks beating you up on the way home.

"I'm not getting bullied," I said, squirming slightly in my seatbelt. Thankfully, my voice was pretty much under control by this point.

And anyway, I wasn't exactly lying. As far as I can understand it, bullies usually threaten you or nick your dinner money, or something. The Lowfield boys just punched me in the face and wandered off. I wasn't sure if that counted.

"You've got to stand up to bullies, Dylan," said my dad, flicking me a glance in the rear-view mirror.

"Don't *you* start," said Mum, turning on him this time. "That's how fights get started. If anyone's threatening you, Dylan, you should go straight to a teacher."

"I'm *fine*," I insisted, going into a sulkier voice than I thought was strictly necessary and sinking back into the seat as if I could stop Mum from talking to me just by avoiding eye contact. "Nobody's bullying me. . ."

"This is the one," said my dad, stopping the car in front of a tiny terraced house.

I hadn't been to see Lennon at uni before, but I knew he'd spent his first year in flats owned by the university. Before the summer holiday, though, he'd announced that it'd be cheaper for him to share a house with his mates. And looking at his house . . . well, I wasn't exactly surprised that it was a money-saving option. After all, I had trouble picturing many people wanting to live in a house with beer cans in the garden and a board instead of one of the panes of glass that ought to have been in the door. Then again, it *was* only two doors away from a chip shop, so Lennon probably snapped it up.

"Heyyy!" shouted Lennon, appearing at the door and looking delighted to see us, despite the fact that, from the state of his hair, it looked like he'd just woken up – possibly after a night sleeping in a hedge. "Come on in! Anyone fancy a cup of tea?"

Lennon, by the way, needs about six cups of tea a day just to function. If he was the person threatening me, I wouldn't need to worry about learning chokeholds or armlocks to immobilize him – I'd just steal his kettle.

"How's the eye, Dylan?" asked Lennon, leaning in and trying to poke at it. Honestly, why do people feel the need to *do* that? "What happened again?"

"Cricket ball," I said, leaning away. "And it's fine. How's the wrist?"

"OK," said Lennon, quickly, keeping his hand as far away from Mum and Dad as he possibly could. I was too far away to make out any of the scribble on his grimy-looking cast, but I would've bet there were some words on there that he didn't want them seeing.

We all crowded through the narrow hallway, trying not to snag any clothing on the mountain bike leaning against the wall. Lennon carried on into the house's tiny kitchen, where we could still see him as we tried to arrange ourselves on the battered sofa and chairs.

"Nice, um, house," said my mum, eyeing the collection of posters on the walls. She probably liked the ones of Steve McQueen and Bob Dylan. She might even have approved of the one of Albert Einstein – even though he had his tongue sticking out. The picture of Kylie scratching her bum, though? That got a definite frown.

"I'd have thought," said my dad, tracing a finger along the TV screen and leaving a clear trail in the dust covering it, "that you might have tidied up before we arrived."

"I did," said Lennon, sniffing a carton of milk, making a face and sticking it back in the fridge. I glanced around at the cups stacked up in the sink and the bulging sack of empty beer cans propped up next to the bin and decided it was probably a good job we hadn't arrived ten minutes early.

"So, how's it going?" Lennon shouted from the kitchen, catapulting a tea bag towards the swing-top bin with a flick of his spoon. It missed, hit the wall with a wet thud and slid down to rest on the floor. Lennon ignored it. Mum winced, but didn't say anything.

Dad cleared his throat. "Fine, thank you, Lennon. How's the course?"

Lennon flinched, and the next tea bag didn't even make it to the wall, splattering across the floor with a thump.

"Fine," said Lennon. "Great. Hard work, you know, but still basically OK."

"What've you been studying recently?"

"Politics."

"We know that, Lennon. What *sort* of politics?"

"Just . . . politics. You know, Tony Blair, Socrates, John Stuart Mill. Politics."

I could see that the parents weren't too impressed with this obvious bit of bluffing, but before either of them could say anything, there was a thudding on the stairs and Lennon got a reprieve. Well, sort of.

"Oh, my f. . . Aarrgh! Hello," said the huge,

confused-looking man in the doorway. He crinkled up his forehead and squeezed himself on to the room's smallest chair. "Morning, Lennon," he shouted towards the kitchen, trying to arrange his boxer shorts so that the person opposite him (my horrified-looking mum) wouldn't see anything – ahem – unfortunate.

"Morning, Steve!" shouted Lennon from the kitchen. "Family, this is Big Steve. Steve, this is my family. Fancy a cup of tea?"

"Yeah," croaked Steve, wincing. "Sorry, I'm feeling a bit fragile this morning."

"That's all right," said my mum, not looking impressed. "Are you on Lennon's course?"

"What?" Steve crumpled up his face again. Obviously, whatever he'd done the night before wasn't having the best effect on his thought processes. "You mean am I doing—"

"Tea's up!" interrupted Lennon, manoeuvring a tray into the living room. "No, Steve's doing biochemistry, Mum. Not politics."

"Right," mumbled Steve. "Not politics."

"Thanks, Lennon," said my dad, taking the steaming cup of tea with the least number of brown trickles down the side. "By the way, whose is that?"

We all looked in the direction he was pointing. There, at the end of the kitchen, propped against a wall, was a gleaming unicycle. There was a pause.

Big Steve blinked once, hard, then said: "Mine."

There was another, slightly shorter pause. I expect everyone was doing the same as me – that is, trying to picture this huge bloke wobbling about on a one-wheeled bike. It took a bit of imagination, I have to say.

"Really?" asked my mum, probably the only person diplomatic enough to respond without giggling. "That's . . . nice."

"Sorry, Lennon, how *exactly* did you break your wrist, again?" asked my dad.

"Fell down the stairs," said Lennon quickly, taking a swig of boiling-hot tea and obviously struggling to gulp it down.

"Were you drunk?"

"No!" insisted Lennon. There was a pause. "Well, a little bit."

There were tuts and frowns from everyone, except for Steve, who seemed to be concentrating on focusing on one very specific bit of carpet as the conversation moved on. At one point, I thought I saw his cheeks bulge as if he was doing that thing where you throw up in your mouth and swallow it, but I wouldn't swear to that in court, or anything. And then, out of nowhere, came the bombshell.

"Is it all right if Dylan stays here tonight, Lennon?" asked my mum. "We've only got a twin room at the hotel, and I'm sure he'd rather spend some more time with his big brother, anyway. . ."

"Sure!" said Lennon, seeming suspiciously cheerful. "He can sleep on the couch!"

I glanced at the couch. It looked like it *already* had things sleeping in it. I could imagine it was once like Dec's mum's puke-patterned sofa, but time, spillages and Big Steve had battered it into a floppy, flowery mess.

"Hang on a minute. . ." I started.

"Sorry, Dylan, but it's either that or you sleep on the floor at the Travelodge," said Mum.

"Don't worry, Dylan, it'll be cool." Lennon nodded, enthusiastically.

"OK," I groaned. OK, so the sofa wasn't the most appealing option, but it *definitely* beat listening to my dad snore. . .

"Great!" My mum smiled, brightening up.

"Now, hurry up, and we can all go for a look at the university!"

"The . . . university?" said Lennon, suddenly looking like he'd gulped down more tea than he could swallow. . .

"And that building's, um . . . something to do with biology. I think. . ." Lennon trailed off uncertainly.

Yawn. Getting a guided tour of Birmingham University probably wouldn't have been much fun even at the best of times – after all, it's just a lot of big red buildings – but with my brother acting as the world's least knowledgeable tour guide, I was beginning to wish I'd stayed on the sofa, watching Steve try to keep his digestive system in order. Mum was doing her best to show an interest, trying to get excited about bits of interesting architecture and asking lots of questions, but Dad looked about as mind-numbed as I felt. In fact, I was just about to suggest we go to sit in the car with the windows rolled up when something interesting happened.

"Hey, Lennon!" squeaked an excited-looking, ginger-haired girl, dashing up to us with an armful of books. "What are *you* doing here?"

"Hi, um, Laura," said Lennon, still looking uncomfortable. We'd been out of the house for at least two hours, and my big brother still looked like one of the newborn puppies from *Animal Hospital,* all confused and blinking in direct sunlight. "How're you?"

"Great," squeaked the girl – honestly she sounded like she was on helium, or something, "I haven't seen you for ages!"

"Well, I've been spending a lot of time in the library." Lennon shrugged. "Y'know, second year and everything – time to do some work –"

"But what're you doing up here? I thought you'd. . ."

". . .broken my wrist, yeah," Lennon finished, quickly. "I'm just here to show my mum and dad around, then I'm going back home. Mum, Dad, this is Laura."

"Hi," said my dad, giving Laura an approving look.

"Nice to meet you," said my mum, glaring at my dad.

"Oh. Right!" said the girl, as if she'd only just noticed Mum and Dad standing there. "Nice to meet you! Well, I'll leave you to it. Byeee!"

"She seemed nice, Lennon," said my mum.

"Who was she?"

"Hmm?" said Lennon, looking distracted. "Oh, just a friend of mine."

But then the weird thing happened – Lennon turned around and actually *winked* at me. And, yep, even though I hadn't thought of it before, suddenly my brother seemed like the *perfect* person to talk to. . .

"Lennon?" I said, trying to lever myself up off the sofa. "Have you ever been stuck in the friend zone?"

We'd just spent a *very* awkward couple of hours in a pizza restaurant in the centre of town, with my mum and dad relentlessly quizzing Lennon about:

a) How his course was going.

b) Whether he was drinking too much, and. . .

c) Whatever happened to that lovely Lucy girl? (To be fair, this was mostly my mum).

It was like the police interrogations you see on TV, except with garlic bread. Lennon did his best to stay calm by necking about half a bottle of red wine, although he looked pretty relieved whenever the waitress came by and interrupted all the questioning. He looked worn out.

"Hmm?" said Lennon, sipping his sixth cup of tea of the day and not taking his eyes off the TV.

Sigh. I tried again.

"Well. . ." I said. "I mean, was that girl today, like, one of your exes, or what?"

"Oh, her!" Lennon said, brightly. "No, I'm just friends with her."

"Right," I said, feeling like I was getting somewhere.

"Although," Lennon sipped his tea again. "I might have snogged her once. There was this party, and. . ." He trailed off, looking lost in pleasant memories. *Sigh.*

"So when you're, erm, trying to . . . you know, with girls. . ." I started, a bit uncertainly.

"You mean when I'm *after* one? Yeah."

"Are you friends with them first, or what? Or is that not the right, um. . ."

Lennon took another swig of tea and looked like he was deep in some sort of caffeine-based meditation. Finally, he said, "Do you mean, 'have I ever been friends with a girl I didn't fancy'?"

"Erm. . ." That wasn't *exactly* the question I'd been aiming at.

"Because the answer's no."

"But. . ."

"Well, probably not, anyway," Lennon carried on, thoughtfully. "But that's a bit weird, isn't it? I mean, I'm mates with Big Steve, but I'm not *attracted* to him. Hmm."

This had to be the wine, I decided.

"So you haven't got any girl mates?"

"Yeah, I've got loads," Lennon said, brightly. "But I think they're mostly ones I fancied for a bit, then hung out with, then never did anything about, then sort of ended up friends with." He paused, as if he was seriously thinking about something. "Hang on, I've just remembered – Steve left some beer hidden in the cupboard under the sink! Brilliant!"

And Lennon was off, back to watching TV and cracking open his flatmate's stash of cheap lager. And leaving me *very* confused – I mean, if *he'd* ended up in the Friendship Circle with "loads" of girls, had I already left it too late with Kate?

Broke . . . in More Ways than One

"Dylan!"

"Hwuh?" I tried to blink the sleep out of my eyes. To be fair, I'd slept pretty well on the sofa. Once you got used to the musty smell, it was just like a big cocoon, the broken springs meaning you sort of sank *into* it rather than lying on top. It was actually pretty comfy. Of course, it didn't help when Big Steve got in at two in the morning and decided to make himself some Marmite on toast – which, bizarrely, seemed to involve clattering every single plate in the kitchen against each other – but I'd slept OK. That is, until my brother decided to wake me up at. . . "Er, what time is it?"

"Seven-ish. Brought you a cup of tea. I need to talk to you."

"About what?" I asked, suspiciously. Cups of tea are one thing, but Lennon waking up before midday? Something had to be seriously wrong.

"I'm out of cash," said Lennon, totally straight-faced. No "you-know-me" smirk, no "hey, check out my crazy student life!" grin – this was Lennon at the most serious I've ever seen him. "I dunno what to do."

Lennon's money-making schemes are legendary. Everybody remembers the time he rang Dad for a lift home from Bristol police station – not because he'd been caught trying to rob a bank, but because he'd discovered that they'd pay ten pounds a time to the people who make up the numbers in a line-up. Unfortunately, he sort of scuppered that one by dying his hair to impress a goth girl he liked – as the police pointed out, there aren't *that* many purple-haired bank robbers around. Then there was the time he was all set to volunteer for some sort of experimental drugs-testing – obviously, Mum put a stop to that, even though my sister announced that she was finally in favour of testing on dumb animals. And, of course, there was the time he found out that it's actually possible to sell your own . . . well, let's not go into that one. Basically, Lennon'll do absolutely *anything* to make some cash quick – as long as he doesn't have to get a job. And that's sort of the problem.

"Usually, I'd go out busking," explained Lennon, looking mournfully into his own tea. "But obviously, I've got this broken wrist thing going on at the moment."

"Busking?" I was gobsmacked. Even by the standards of the buskers I've seen around Bristol city centre, I couldn't imagine Lennon actually earning money for . . . well, anything, really. He knows about three chords on the guitar, and he just *adapts* any song he wants to play to them. He definitely can't sing, and as for dancing – well, he's pretty good at that, but only when he's drunk enough beer to kill an elephant. Nope, the only thing I could see my brother doing is being one of those blokes who paint themselves grey and pretend to be statues – and even then, he'd never be able to stay still without a cup of tea for more than about ten minutes. Unless you left him on a sofa.

"Look," I carried on, "can't you just ask Mum and Dad? They can probably sort something out. . ."

Realistically, though, I felt a bit bad for suggesting it. Mum had enough to worry about with inspectors and, um, me, and Dad . . . well, Dad'd probably just tell Lennon to stop drinking so much. I doubted Lennon wanted that to happen very much. He looked gloomy.

"Yeah, after I've just blown forty quid on a second-hand unicycle?"

"What?"

"What?" said Lennon, sounding defensive. "It seemed like a bargain at the time, but they're bloody difficult to ride, and I got on this hill, and. . ."

Lennon waved his wrist-cast at me, apologetically. I'd like to say I was surprised, but this was *just* the sort of thing my brother's famous for.

"Shouldn't you be spending your money on books or something?"

That got a blank look. Eventually, Lennon said, "Yes. Yes, Dylan, I ought to be spending my money on books. But, erm, is there any way you could lend me some cash?"

"Ahh. . ."

"It's just for a couple of weeks."

"Um. . ."

"There's always the grandma fund. . ."

Ah. So *that* was what Lennon was thinking. For years, our gran's been giving us the odd fiver whenever we go to visit her – well, Lennon doesn't get them any more, but you get the idea. And every time – every single time – our mum and dad insist that we put them in the bank straight away. Hence – "The Grandma Fund".

"Erm. . ."

"I'll pay you back as soon as I can start performing again."

This was too much. "Look," I said, putting my foot down. "Can't you just rack up a student loan like everyone else?"

"It's a bit more complicated than that, Dylan," said Lennon, nervously.

"Why?" I said. "You're a student, aren't you?"

"Yeah. . ." said Lennon. "But . . . that stuff takes *ages* to sort out, and I'm *really* strapped for cash."

"Yeah, but. . ." I was weakening. Lennon must've sensed it.

"Pleeeeease, Dylan."

"But . . . hang on. . ."

"Come on, mate."

"I'll . . . see what I can do."

"Cheers, Dylan!" Lennon brightened up immediately, bounced out of his seat and slapped me on the back. "I *knew* you'd help out. Now, how about another cup of tea?"

Fortunately, some very loud people in the room next to theirs at the Travelodge meant Mum and Dad were even more worn out than me in the morning – they barely even had the strength to give Lennon the usual orders about doing more work and going out less before we left. It was a good thing for me, too – if they'd been more alert, they might have noticed that I spent most of the two-hour drive back to Bristol staring broodily out of the window, thinking about the mess Lennon had just dropped me in. I felt bad for him, but it *was* his own fault. Still, there was *one* other person I could count on for sensible advice.

"Becky," I started, pushing open her bedroom door, and immediately being hit by a blast of music from the Manics – Becky's favourite "angry" band. "I need to talk to you about. . ."

I froze.

It wasn't Becky and Charlie's *position* that gave them away, exactly. I mean, they *were* sitting pretty close together on Becky's bed, almost as if they'd had just enough time to, erm, break contact when they saw the door open – but hey, that could've been totally innocent. It wasn't even really Charlie, whose expression went from "mildly surprised" straight back to "totally cheerful" almost before I had chance to notice it. Nope, what really gave the game away was Becky, whose expression went from "embarrassed" through "flustered" to "absolutely terrifyingly furious" in about two seconds. Honestly, it was like watching someone flick through channels on a TV. I think I was pretty brave not to just run for it.

"Don't you *knock*, Dylan?" she finally managed, probably deciding against adding, "I'm going to kill you" thanks to Charlie being there. Homicidal tendencies in a girlfriend? *So* not attractive.

"Sorry," I said. "I will next time."

Too right. Sisters snogging is like cows giving birth or something – you know it has to happen, it's just that you never want to actually *see* it.

"What's up, man?" asked Charlie, looking more and more amused every second. I didn't mind, though – this wasn't the superior sort of half-smile, half-sneer Spider used to give me when he was lounging around on Becky's bed. In fact, it was more like the smirk you give your mate when a teacher's going mental at you both. I was liking Charlie more and more.

"Um, I just wanted to say hi," I managed, weakly. Becky was one thing, but I couldn't go sharing our family's financial woes with a complete stranger, even if he seemed like a nice guy.

"Er, hi. . ." said Charlie, giving me a confused wrinkle of his eyebrows and a little wave.

"And good*bye*," snarled Becky, clearing the distance from the bed to the door in less than a second and half-slamming it in my face. And leaving me with more problems than I started with – I mean, Lennon was one thing, but then there was the friend zone to think about. Charlie seemed to have managed to get out of it – even Spider managed it with a face full of metal and a permanently stroppy attitude – so why couldn't I?

Be Tough, Dec, be Tough...

"Hwoooaaa. . ."

It was Monday. It was breaktime. And it looked as if the stress was finally getting to Dec.

"It's called the crane kick," he was explaining to a group of awed-(and not-so-awed)-looking Year Sevens, "there's no defence against it."

He was posing on one leg, on one of the metal benches riveted into the floor around the playground.

"It looks a bit dangerous. . ." said one of the Year Sevens, nervously.

"Yeah, I don't want any of you trying it," said Dec. "It takes perfect balance and years of training."

"It's not even a proper kick!" pointed out one

of the more confident Year Sevens. "I do tae kwon do!"

Honestly, kids today – no respect. When I was a Year Seven, I could hardly speak to anyone from the years above, let alone give them attitude. Dec wobbled slightly.

"You probably just haven't been taught it yet. . ." he said, not sounding quite so arrogant.

"Go on, then," said the cocky-looking Year Seven, folding his arms and watching expectantly. I'd have given him a slap around the back of the head for being cheeky, but he was almost as big as me.

"OK. . ." said Dec, shuffling slightly. "Hyaaah!"

And he jumped.

You know when Michael Buerk interviews people who've been in car crashes and they say they felt like the whole thing happened in slow motion? I don't think that's true – I think the whole situation's just so horrible that you pay extra attention and see everything in really clear detail. Or at least, that's what I felt like when I saw Dec jump off the bench. For a second, I really thought he was going to make it – he flicked a kick out with his back leg, and just managed to land back on the bench.

Unfortunately, his regulation-black, flat-soled school shoes didn't exactly grip the bench properly. If only he'd been wearing his ultra-trendy skate trainers, everything might have been different. . .

"Owww!" yelped Dec, *just* missing his unmentionables as his thigh slammed into the bench. The Year Sevens scattered, obviously a bit unnerved by the way his face was twisting up in pain. Or at least, most of them did – the cocky one made a little "tch" noise under his breath and strolled off without a care in the world.

"All right, mate?" I said, sitting down on the bench next to him.

"Noo-www," squeaked Dec, in a voice that seemed slightly higher than normal. Honestly, if I had a camcorder I'd *never* have to worry about money – I'd just follow him around, video all the stupid stuff he does, send the tapes to *You've Been Framed* and wait for the cash to roll in.

"Good weekend?"

"All right," he breathed, sounding a bit healthier this time. "Got a couple more messages from the stalker. They're sort of getting angrier, and she's stopped putting the little Xs on them now. What about you?"

"Went to my brother's," I said.

"Yeah?" Dec looked suddenly interested. "Did he take you out anywhere?"

"Not really," I mumbled, not sure whether to tell Dec about my brother's money worries.

"Being a student must be sweet," sighed Dec. "You never have to do any work. . ."

"So how's that different from your life now?" I grinned at him. OK, cheap shot. Dec punched me in the arm.

"Are *you* the kid that got thumped by the Lowfield boys?" interrupted a wide-looking boy I recognized as a Year Ten.

"Erm, yeah. . ." I started, resisting the urge to add "what do *you* think, genius? I'm the only one here with a black eye". Year Tens hate that stuff.

"What's your name?"

"Um, Dylan."

"Right," said the Year Ten. "Don't worry about it, Dylan."

"OK," I said. "Erm, why not?"

"Because we're gonna sort the Lowfield lot out," said the Year Ten, with a little sneer.

And he was off again, doing that sort of slouched walk that makes it look like you've got an invisible roll of carpet under each arm.

"What was *that* about?" I asked.

"Search me." Dec shrugged. "But it sounds like there's going to be trouble. . ."

The Art of Fighting Without Fighting

"Boards . . . don't hit back!" snarled Bruce Lee, just before showing some beardy bloke why he'd have been better off sticking to fighting bits of wood. I smiled. I was home before everyone else, and there's something quite nice about watching people get beaten up when you know you don't have to get involved.

I flopped down on the sofa and thought about all the stuff I had to worry about. Which, I reckoned, went in about this order:

1) Fighting. OK, so everyone thinks about being a badass some time, don't they? I mean, you see a documentary about Shaolin monks, and there're seven year olds on it who can do backflips and smash concrete with their heads and things, and for a second you think:

brilliant! Why didn't my mum and dad send me to a monastery in China instead of forcing me to waste ten years of my life learning about prime numbers and how to ask for directions in German? But realistically, I think I was happier with a cup of tea and a packet of biscuits than doing press-ups on my knuckles and sprinting up mountains. After last week's Aiki-jitsu class, I wasn't sure I could handle another session, let alone however many lessons it'd take to become a killing machine. But if I couldn't, then my only option was problem. . .

2) The Idiots. It looked like they were gearing up for some sort of inter-school war with Lowfield, with me stuck right in the middle. And then there was. . .

3) Lennon. Trust my idiot brother to expect me to sort out his life for him.

4) My fancy dress outfit. The way I was feeling, I might have to go for Dec's bear idea. Then at least I could pretend to be staying in character when I didn't talk to anybody.

5) Dec's Friendship Circle theory. I couldn't work it out. I mean, if you had to worry about getting stuck in the Friendship Circle, you

couldn't ever be friends with anybody. But if you couldn't be friends with anybody, how could you work out who you really liked? Were you supposed to go from not-talking to full-speed-ahead and just *hope* that you ended up with someone you liked? No, because look what happened with Fiona – the weird skater girl I'd somehow half ended up with at my cousin's wedding. But then, look at Dec and The Stalker – maybe that was just something you had to put up with. And look at my brother. And Matt. And. . . then the doorbell rang.

"Hey," said Charlie, slouching in the doorway in his jumper. It was weird – he had that same sort of laid-back way of talking as Spider (grrr), but he didn't annoy me half as much. "Is Becky in?"

"Nope," I said. "But you can wait, if you want."

"Thanks, man," Charlie drawled, following me through into the living room. "Feels like I've been walking for – hey! *Enter the Dragon*!"

"Yeah, it's part of my brother's collection," I explained.

"Cool film, man," Charlie said, slumping into a

chair. "Hey, Becky was telling me you're into this stuff yourself."

"Not really," I said, a bit embarrassed. I could just *imagine* what Becky had said about me learning to beat people up. "What else has she told you?"

"Not much, man," said Charlie. "Hey, sorry about the other day."

"Yeah," I said. "But . . . I thought you were just *mates*?"

"We are," said Charlie, looking a bit confused. "Haven't you ever been mates with a girl you've ended up going out with?"

"Erm. . ." I said, a bit too embarrassed to tell this cool-seeming bloke that I hadn't been out with anyone, ever. I mean, the closest I've ever come to actually snogging someone is, erm, getting puked on at my cousin's wedding. Instead, I tried, "So how do I get out of the friend zone?"

"The what?" Now Charlie looked *really* confused.

"Well, like, how do I go from being friends to . . . you know," I shuffled uncomfortably. "I mean, how did *you* go from being mates with to, um. . ." I trailed off, not wanting to say "snogging my sister". Euch.

"Erm. . ." Charlie was starting to go bright red. "It just . . . sort of . . . happened."

"*What* just sort of happened?" said Becky, standing in the doorway.

Silent, but Deadly...

I didn't think there were too many things more uncomfortable than your sister catching you talking to her new boyfriend about how they got together, but on Tuesday, I found out there were actually quite a few. First, obviously, there was the walk home. And things only got worse from there...

"More lemonade, boys?" asked Will's mum, holding out a tray of glasses of . . . something that looked more like used bath water than the fizzy pop you get out of vending machines.

We don't meet up round at Will's house very often. It's not that it's too far away, or anything – it's just that, well, I always feel like I have to be in Super-Polite Best Behaviour mode whenever his mum's around. She never actually *says* anything, but she's always giving me these suspicious looks, as if she half expects me to start nicking the ornaments or forcing Will to smoke as soon as her back's turned. It's not exactly a relaxing way to spend your free time, especially when she keeps bursting in to offer you her home-made drinks. Still, Will reckoned she was starting to get suspicious about the fact that he'd suddenly started playing "badminton", and if he disappeared off to someone else's house it'd only make things worse.

"Thanks, Mum," said Will, helping himself to a glass.

"Yes, please," I said, inwardly groaning. When Will's mum says "lemonade', she means "lemon-flavoured water". It tastes like she's forgotten to put the sugar in, and it gives your teeth a strange sort of fuzzy tinge every time you drink it. Still, you've got to be polite, haven't you?

"No thank you, Mrs Rogerson." Dec was frowning over a complicated-looking book of equations, absent-mindedly tapping a pencil against his paper. "So if N equals negative two, then X must be. . ."

He scribbled something down. Will's mum beamed at him.

"Well, I can see you're all working very hard – I'll leave you to it."

"Bye, Mrs Rogerson," said Dec, still not looking up from his work as she backed out of the room and closed the door.

I took a swig of lemonade, and winced.

"I don't know how you can drink that stuff." Dec flung his book away with a disgusted look. "It makes my teeth hurt."

"You can talk," I said, putting on my best fake-posh voice. "No thank you, Mrs Rogerson. Bye-bye, Mrs Rogerson. No, I'd *never* take your son to kung-fu lessons without telling you, Mrs Rogerson."

"It's not funny," Will groaned, chucking his own book on the floor. "If she finds out I'm fighting *and* I lied to her about it, I'm grounded *for ever.* I'm not sure how long I'm going to be able to get away with 'playing badminton' twice a week."

"Just give it a couple more lessons and you'll be a killing machine," Dec suggested. "I mean, they'll probably move on to some sort of ninja death touch on Friday."

"Well, that move we learnt the other day's a bit like the Vulcan nerve grip. . ." Will started.

"Yeah, except the Vulcan death grip knocks people out," Dec pointed out. "That move we did just makes them go 'Ow!' until you have to let go, and then they can kick your head in."

"It's a shame you can't just programme it straight into your brain in ten minutes, like in *The Matrix*," I said. "That'd be brilliant!"

"D'you think the people in *The Matrix* learn everything like that?" Dec asked, reading my mind. "I mean, imagine if you could just learn ten years' worth of geography and science and stuff by just going –" He did a quick impression of Keanu Reeves juddering his head around "– you'd never have to go to school again!"

"Or you could be amazing at football. . ." I said, getting quite into the idea.

"Or skateboarding," added Dec.

"Or, um, tap dancing," Will tried to join in – I really worry about him, sometimes.

"Or badminton. . ." carried on Dec, with an evil little smirk. Will looked as if he'd just been told he only had a week to live.

"Anyway!" I interrupted, changing the subject as quickly as possible. "What are we doing about Friday?"

"*Friday,*" groaned Dec. "I'd forgotten about Friday."

"Hey, it's a party. . ." I said, slightly weakly.

"You're only saying that because it's your *girlfriend's,*" Dec moaned. "I can't believe you haven't come up with anything to impress her yet."

"Yeah?" I said. "Well, *I* can't believe you've spent the past week running away from *your* girlfriend."

"She's a nutcase!"

"I, um, had one idea," Will suddenly piped up, rummaging around in a drawer, "I found it on the internet. . ."

"Oh, great," muttered Dec. "We're all going to go as nerds."

Will ignored him, and pulled out a perfectly ironed black T-shirt. Whatever this plan involved, I was almost sure that his mum wasn't going to approve.

"First, you need a T-shirt," he explained. "It doesn't matter if it's got a logo on, or anything, because you just turn it inside out and put it on your head, like this."

Will stood there with his face poking out of the head-hole in his spare T-shirt, wearing it –

I suppose – a *little* bit like a nun. I got the impression we were supposed to be impressed.

"You can see the label," pointed out Dec.

"Yeah, but I haven't finished yet," Will carried on. "Then you tie the sleeves behind the back of your head, and—"

"And you look like you've got a T-shirt tied to your head," Dec interrupted.

"Yeah. . ." said Will. "But then you fold the collar round like this, and *then* you tuck the bottom bit up around your nose, and. . ."

He did a little pose, ending with a Keanu Reeves-style "come on, then" hand-flick. I'm sure it would've been more impressive if he hadn't overbalanced and landed on his bed.

"Brilliant!" I said, sitting up.

"Hey, yeah, that *is* pretty good," Dec said, finally looking impressed. "Nice one, Will-san."

So that was settled, then. We might not know anything about kung fu, but we were going to fancy dress Friday as warriors of the night. As shadowy assassins. As the deadliest people alive. As . . . ninjas!

"Erm, are there actually any films with ninjas in?" asked Dec.

"Yeah!" I said, enthusiastically, thinking of

Lennon's collection. "There's *American Ninja,* and *Revenge of the Ninja,* and that sequel to *Revenge of the Ninja.*"

"Oh yeah," said Dec, "*Return of the Ninja.* That one was great. . ." He cocked his head to one side as if he was listening for something, "Hey, is that your mum coming up the stairs?"

"Whfff?" squeaked Will, trying to yank the hood off his head, getting it stuck halfway over his eyes and smashing one of his shins into his bed as he hopped around in panic. "Wrrrgh!"

So much for silent but deadly. . .

Just Good Friends?

"Lennon rang while you were out, Dylan." My mum actually sounded pleased, even though she was looking up from another mammoth pile of reports and books. Not surprising, really – a phone call from Lennon's like getting a letter from the pope. Better, actually, since my mum isn't religious and worries about my brother *constantly*. "He said he wanted to talk to you."

"'K," I said, ditching my bags. When I got to the phone, though, I saw something I hadn't exactly been expecting.

"Yeah . . . yeah. . ." Becky was saying. Nothing special there, but it's been a while since I've seen my sister smiling – y'know, *really* smiling. I mean, she gets an evil smirk on her face sometimes, but that's not the same as the puppy-dog, goofy grin she had on at this particular moment. Of course, that all changed when she saw me.

"'Scuse me. . . *Get lost!* . . .Sorry about that." The "get lost" bit was snarled in my general direction, but then Becky went straight back to that smile. And – get this – she was twirling her hair. Unbelievable. I did the polite thing, which was – obviously – to lurk around in the general background, then pounce as soon as she hung up.

"Mmm . . . yeah . . . bye," Becky said, hanging up the phone with a little *click* instead of her traditional slam-the-handset-down movement.

"Who was that?" I said, resisting my natural little-brother urge to make smoochy noises and flutter my eyelashes at her.

"None of your business," said Becky. "But it was Charlie."

Like I said – unbelievable.

"I thought he was just your mate," I said.

"Yeah, we've been mates for ages," said Becky, a bit huffily, "but. . . Well, it's none of your business."

I'd always thought that if I actually *asked* Becky for advice on what to do about Kate, she'd probably mumble something about aromatherapy or meditation or something. But right at this moment, it seemed like a really good idea.

"So are you two going out, or what?" I said. "Or, I mean. . ."

"Maybe," said Becky, and then did something she does even less often than smiling properly – she actually went *pink*.

"That's brilliant!" I said – and, surprisingly, I really meant it. Apart from practically guaranteeing me a couple of weeks of sisterly friendliness, I knew now that being in the friend zone didn't *necessarily* mean giving up on kissing Kate ever. Becky still looked bewildered, so while she was still too surprised to react, I gave her a little hug.

"Er, thanks," she said, still trying to work out whether I was being sarcastic as I dashed off up the stairs. It wasn't like I needed the phone, really – I knew what Lennon wanted. And, considering that I was in the best mood I'd been in for days, he'd just have to wait. . .

Seeing Red

"Why do you want to study Aiki-jitsu?" was the last question on the sheet of paper. I tapped my biro on my teeth and thought about it.

It was Wednesday. German lessons aside, the day had flown by. It was time for Aiki-jitsu – again. Will had brought his badminton racket – again. And, yes, Dec had forgotten to bow before he strolled on to the mat, and ended up with extra press-ups to do . . . again.

It wasn't *all* the same, though. Instead of going straight on to bending each other into uncomfortable positions, Sensei Moody called us all to one side and told us that, if we were really serious about training, we'd need to fill in membership forms. Which was sort of a problem. For a start, Will panicked when he got to the bit about an "emergency telephone number" – and he wasn't entirely calmed down when Dec pointed out that, if he got his arm broken, his mum'd be far too stressed out to bother shouting at him. Then there was this. Why did I want to learn to fight? Hmm.

I couldn't put "To beat up some kids who're hassling me" – that much was obvious. I thought about something like "To achieve inner peace and tranquillity", but decided that was a bit too much like something Becky might say. I even thought about just putting "Because I've seen loads of Jackie Chan films", but that sounded a bit too flippant. Finally, I settled on "To get fit and meet new people" – a massive cop-out, since that was what had been written on the flyer. Looking over Will's shoulder, I noticed that he'd had the same idea – he'd written, "To gain confidence and learn to defend myself". Dec, on the other hand, wasn't going to take the easy way out – he'd printed in capital letters, "To avenge my master, who was killed by a rival kung-fu school". Sensei Moody made a sort of "humph" noise when he handed it in, but just as it looked like he was about to order Dec to spend the rest of the lesson doing press-ups, there was a shout from the doorway.

"Sorry I'm late, *sensei*!"

We looked over. And there, standing statue-straight in a freshly ironed gi . . . was Gary Pierce.

"Hey, Dylan, that's not. . ." Will trailed off, as GP looked straight at us.

"I've gone right off this 'meeting new people' stuff," Dec whispered.

The rest of the lesson was a sort of good news/bad news situation. The good news was, we didn't have to go near GP. He was a yellow belt – only one grade higher than white, but still enough to put him in a different group from the three of us, practising advanced arm-twisting techniques while we flopped about doing forward rolls.

The bad news was, it looked like he was even more of a psycho than we'd thought. Occasionally there was an extra-loud thump on the mats or a muffled "waaargh!" noise from another bit of the floor, and every time we looked over, there was GP, giving some poor yellow-belt the same insane stare I'd seen him giving Dec. And the even worse news was, he'd recognized us, too. He kept glancing over with his grim, tunnel-vision look, and we all had to keep glancing away really quickly and pretending to be trying to work out some lock or other. Once or twice, it looked like he was about to come over and say – or do – something, but he never got the opportunity while Sensei Moody was milling about.

"Ya-me!" yelled Moody, after what felt more like a year than an hour and a half. "Line up. We're going to do some self-defence."

I glanced at Dec and Will, who were both looking nervous.

"Self-defence is all about personal space," Moody carried on, holding up his hands with a pair of glove-style pads on. "If someone invades your personal space, they're probably going to fight you anyway, so hold your hands out like this." He put his arms out in front of him in a calm-down, nothing-to-get-excited-about pose. "And then you're defining your own personal space. If he comes into that space, then you want to get the first punch in."

"I'm not sure that counts as self-defence," muttered Dec.

"No talking," barked Moody. "Now, I don't want you lads doing this at school, mind." He gave us a stern look, then he winked. "You'll get me in trouble."

We shuffled along in a line, holding out our hands, then smacking the pads as soon as they were in range.

"OK, come on. . . That's right. . . Now *hit it*! Not hard enough! Harder! Put your shoulder into it!" Trevor Moody was shouting at people. "You're telegraphing it too much! Useless!" GP was three people ahead of me in the line, but he didn't look round. When it came to his go, he strolled up to the front looking like he was out for a stroll in the park, then smashed into the pad with a THWACK that made me wince.

"Good innocent expression," said Moody, giving GP a grin. "He'd never have seen that coming."

Finally, it was my go. I walked up to the pad with my most innocent expression on and whacked it as hard as I could. Something in my shoulder went *twang*!

"Acceptable," Moody said, as I walked to the back of the line. "That'll do for today. . ."

I clutched my shoulder, which was already starting to throb, as everyone filed out of the class. Then someone tapped me on the shoulder.

"I want a word with you," said Gary Pierce, still staring at me with that super-intense look of his. "I'll see you outside."

Yeah, *right.* Get me outside and do the other eye? No thanks. . .

Then Dec grabbed me.

"We've got to go. Let's get Will. WILL!"

But Will wasn't paying any attention. Instead, he was staring at the little spectators' gallery above the mini-dojo – and he was absolutely white. He looked as if he was about to faint. Then I saw the person Will was scared of, glaring back at him with a look that was even scarier than Gary Pierce's psycho stare. But it *wasn't* Gary Pierce. It wasn't even Sensei Moody. It was Will's mum.

". . .*Never* would have expected it of *you*, William. . ."

To be honest, I wasn't listening to Will's mum that closely.

". . .should have *known* when I saw you sneaking around. . ."

You know when there's nothing you can say, and the only thing to do is stare at the floor, mumble a few apologies and wait for the other person to finish ranting?

". . .and what does that *teacher* think he's playing at? I ought to. . ."

Yeah, listening to Will's mum was a bit like that. To be fair, at least she'd waited until the class was over before she went all volcanic at Will, rather than storming straight on to the mat and swatting Sensei Moody to one side. And yep, it was *sort* of nice of her to offer us a lift home, especially considering that there was a Ginger Psycho waiting for us outside. But if I'd known what the journey home was going to be like, I think I might have taken my chances with GP. . .

". . .seemed like such a *nice* boy. . ."

Dec had got off fairly lightly – partly because his house was closer to the sports centre than mine, but mostly (I suspected) because of the months of sucking up to Will's mum he'd put in already. I was just making a mental note never to be polite about her foul-tasting lemonade again when he hopped out of the car and she *really* started to let rip.

". . .be speaking to your parents about this, I can promise you that," was the last thing I caught, just before Will finally got up the nerve to say something.

"It wasn't Dylan's fault, Mum! It was my

idea. . ." He trailed off. Because that's the problem – although Will's a really good mate and everything, he's really rubbish at standing up to his parents.

"Really?" sniffed Mrs Rogerson, turning her head just enough so that she could look down her nose at me. "I don't know. . . I should have suspected something when I saw him with that eye. . ."

It was all I could do not to jump out of the car and *walk* home. . .

Taking it to the Streets

If Will's mum thought I was a thug just for luring her precious little son to a self-defence class, though, she'd have been absolutely horrified if she knew about my reputation at school. Soon people were going to mistake me for one of the Idiots. Speaking of which. . .

"Where did you get punched, mate?" said Matt, as we got out of the school gates the next day.

"Um, in the eye?" I hazarded, thinking it was a bit obvious. I mean, the bruise was definitely fading, but surely he didn't think my face normally looked like this?

Matt made a little snorting noise, and looked at me like, "How can anyone be so unbelievably stupid and still be able to do up their own shoes in the morning?"

"I meant," he said, "where*abouts*? As in which street."

"Ohhh," I said, suddenly feeling very red. "Just over there."

Great. Now I was making myself look stupid in front of the Idiots.

Matt was leading an assorted group of tough-looking Year Elevens, rugby players, Idiots and slightly scared-looking Year Eights and Nines who'd all "volunteered" to help sort things out with GP and the Lowfield crew. Although I sort of liked the idea of finding GP and making him promise not to thump me – or anybody else – again, I wasn't sure it would be as simple as that. Matt didn't look like he'd be happy with a quick telling-off and a handshake – he looked like he was in it to give someone a serious battering. Meanwhile, my so-called mates had ditched me to deal with the Idiots on my own. OK, so Will was still on probation with his mum, but Dec just *mysteriously* disappeared at the end of the day. I made a mental note to laugh next time he seriously injured himself imitating Jean-Claude Van Damme.

Ten minutes later, with no sign of any Lowfield kids, I was starting to feel even more nervous.

Matt and his big mates were getting grumpy, and although it didn't seem all *that* likely that they'd get really anxious for a fight and start on anyone nearby, I couldn't help at least *considering* it. A couple of Year Eights had obviously had the same idea, mumbling excuses about being late for tea or bored, and sneaking off home. I was just thinking about doing the same, when. . .

"Waaargh!"

There was a sudden shout, then a quick sprint, then a scuffle, then some stuff that sounded like "Get him!" or "Get off!"

"Whoah!" I shouted, shoving my way through the crowd that had suddenly formed. "Pack it in! I mean, erm. . ."

A couple of mean-looking Year Elevens were holding one sullen-looking Lowfield lad, and one slightly scared one, by their shirts, while Matt looked like a general with a couple of prisoners of war. Obviously, none of them were GP, Pizza Boy or Grunty – I mean, what're the odds of getting *exactly* the right Lowfield lads first time?

"Is this them?" demanded Matt.

"Erm, no. . ." I said, apologetically – as if it was *my* fault we'd grabbed the wrong kids.

"Are you sure?" asked Matt. My first reaction

was to say "Yeah, duh, I'm hardly likely to forget them, am I?" – but it looked like he wanted to thump *someone* – and that someone could easily be me.

"Yeah," I said, cautiously. "It's not them. Just leave them, will you?"

"Who's 'them'?" asked the surly-looking Lowfield kid.

"Shut up," spat Matt. "You tell your *mates* that if they want to mess, they know where to find us."

"Who are my mates?" asked the surly kid. Matt looked like he was about to thump him.

"Just leave them!" I almost squeaked. "Go on, it wasn't them. Please."

Matt gave me a looong stare, like "I don't know why I agreed to help such a wimp", then just said:

"I can't believe what a loser you are these days, Dylan."

"Yeah?" I said, suddenly feeling brave. "I can't believe what a *nutter* you are."

"At least I stand up for myself."

"No, you just pick on people," I said, drawing myself up to my full height – still about three inches shorter than Matt, unfortunately. "They weren't anything to do with it."

"They were from Lowfield," said Matt, looking a bit uncomfortable.

"Yeah, but we can't fight *all of Lowfield,*" I insisted. Some of the crowd looked like they were seriously considering it, though. Matt, meanwhile, stared at me again for a looong time, then said: "Sod it. I'm off home."

Phew.

Everyone – apart from a couple of seriously genuine nutters – seemed slightly relieved, and what was left of the Revenge Squad split up and wandered off. I was sort of relieved too, but I couldn't help feeling like I'd just made matters worse. We hadn't stopped GP, we hadn't calmed things down – in fact, the only thing we had done was let Lowfield know that we were looking for a fight. And the worst bit of my evening wasn't even over yet. . .

"Hello?" I shouted at the door, still feeling a bit like a criminal.

The trouble is, everything important and money-related in our house is hidden. Not so that me, Lennon and Becky can't find it, because we've known almost since we were old enough to walk – in Mum and Dad's bedroom there's a cheque book in the sock drawer, an "emergency" twenty-pound note in my mum's copy of *Pride and Prejudice*, and so on – it's more so that, if somebody breaks into the house, they won't be able to go on a spending spree with all our cash. We just have to hope we never get burgled by someone who really likes reading. Or socks.

"Hel-lo?" I said again. Still no answer. Phew.

The trouble is, the little bank-book that'd let me get money out of the Grandma Fund was also in the bedroom – in my mum's drawer. And getting to it without my mum finding out (and asking me lots of awkward questions about why I needed it) meant grabbing it while she wasn't in the house. Which meant doing it now, taking it to the bank at the weekend and (hopefully) replacing it before she noticed it wasn't there any more. Simple. Unfortunately, it turned out to be a bit of a problem.

"Hmm," I said to myself, looking at the drawer.

My mum's one of those people who never throws anything away. In a way, this is great – if you're ever stuck two minutes before somebody's birthday with no wrapping paper, or you desperately need a green biro or a spare button, she's bound to be able to help you out. Unfortunately, it also means that if you want to find something in one of her drawers, you've got to sift through tons of rubbish first – it's like a lucky dip. I yanked open my mum's top drawer, and started rummaging through it, hoping that there wasn't any sort of pattern to the general mess that would be instantly obvious to my eagle-eyed mum. And it *was* a mess: Post-it notes, bits of string, hairclips, odd playing cards, weird foreign coins and . . . *bingo*. There was my bank book. Right between a roll of masking tape and a three-way plug adaptor.

Unfortunately, it was just about that point that I heard the front door slam. I bolted. Shut the bedroom door – quietly – dashed straight through into my room, grabbed a maths book – yeah, *really* unsuspicious, genius – dived on to my bed, and . . . *and I'd left the drawer open.*

There were footsteps on the stairs, and a knock at my door.

"Hello!" I shouted, trying to sound casual and hoping I wasn't sweating.

"Dylan?" said my mum, opening the door and giving me a look I couldn't figure out. This was weird – she hadn't even been in her room yet.

Maybe she'd just seen the guilty expression on my face.

"I thought you had a meeting," I said. Whoops. With all the innocent, non-suspicious things I *could* have said, why did I come out with that?

"It's been postponed till tomorrow," said Mum. "What's the matter, Dylan?"

Honestly, sometimes I can't work out whether mums come with a "something's up" radar, or whether they just say things like "what's the matter?" so often that they're bound to be right some of the time. Either way, I thought it was a bit unnerving.

"I had a look through your drawer," I said. Best get it out in the open, eh? I mean, she was bound to spot it.

"Right," said my mum.

"I was looking for my building society book," I explained – pretty reasonably, I thought.

"Right."

"I thought I'd check how much money I've got in there, if that's OK." I shuffled, uncomfortably. I could feel myself going red, even though I didn't really have anything to feel guilty about. Well, apart from completely skipping over the subject of Lennon's financial difficulties.

Mum looked at me for a long, looong moment.

"I got a phone call from Will's mum today."

"Oh, great," I said.

"Don't be like that."

"Well, what's she been saying about me now?" Why was everyone hassling me? If it wasn't getting punched and then practically accused of going round starting fights, it was my brother stinging me for cash when he was blowing all of his own on second-hand clown kit. And now there was Will's mum. Will's interfering, whinging, dodgy-lemonade-making mum. "I'm sick of her and her, her. . ."

"I've been standing up for you. . ." said my mum, almost apologetically.

"Thanks," I mumbled, getting a quick little flash of guilt.

". . .but I'm worried about you, Dylan. You come home with a black eye, then you announce you're taking up judo. . ."

"Aiki-jitsu," I corrected, very quietly.

". . .then I've got Will's mum telling me you've been encouraging him to lie to her, then I find you going through my drawers. . . If you're in any sort of trouble, Dylan, just *tell* me."

"I'M NOT. . ." I started, then noticed it. I'd heard the edge in her voice, of course I had, but now that I actually looked at her, her eyes looked red. She'd been crying – or at least, *nearly* crying, which is just as bad. And suddenly, I felt like a sulky little kid. "Look – I'm not in any sort of trouble, Mum," I said, trying to sound cheerful. "Sorry if I've been stressing you out recently. There's nothing the matter. I'm fine. Honest."

"Are you sure?" Mum said, giving me her I-want-to-believe-you-but-I-don't face.

"Yeah," I said, not looking her in the eye.

I don't hug my mum all that much. I used to, but you know what it's like – when you hit a certain age, it drops off the cool-things-to-do list even faster than collecting slugs or pretending a cardboard box is a spaceship. But that minute, I gave my mum a big bearhug squeeze, like you do when you're a little kid, even though I'm taller than my mum these days. Mum squeezed back, and yeah, just for a minute, I felt better. Just up until the second I remembered I was lying. About almost everything. . .

The Good Guys Dress in Black...

I was one very moody ninja by Friday evening, on the way to Kate's house. Mum didn't say anything about my choice of outfit, but I got the impression from some sort of mum telepathy (or maybe the complete silence at the dinner table) that she didn't exactly approve of my outfit. I'd managed to dig out a black sweatshirt and some tracksuit bottoms with only a couple of hardly noticeable white stripes down the sides, and the illusion was complete. Dec and Will had done the same. To reduce the danger of attacks from rival ninjas (not very likely, I'll admit) or the Lowfield posse (more worrying), I'd agreed with Dec and Will that we'd meet up near Kate's house and show up together. It should have been brilliant, but maybe it was the adrenaline from Thursday night's fighting, or my (still-throbbing) shoulder injury, or maybe it was that everybody seemed to be ganging up on me, but I was just in the mood for a bit of a scrap. If the Lowfield boys had turned up right then, I'd probably have gone straight for them. In fact, if Chuck Norris himself had jumped out of a tree, with Steven Seagal backing him up, I'd probably have smacked him on the nose. Of course, at least *one* of my fellow shadow warriors wasn't in such a bad mood. . .

"Hwaaaaa!" squealed Dec. He'd somehow made himself a pair of nunchaku out of two toilet rolls and a bit of string, and considering that I've only ever seen them in action during a couple of episodes of *Ninja Turtles*, he seemed to be twirling them about pretty impressively. Well, he was managing to hit Will with them almost as often as he hit himself, anyway.

"Pack it *in*," moaned Will, swatting them away. Unfortunately, he didn't have any toilet rolls to retaliate with, although he *had* cut some throwing stars out of what looked like a cornflakes packet. He threw one at Dec's head, then had to chase after it as the wind whipped it away and into a nearby hedge. I wondered if this was going to carry on all night. . .

As it turned out, it didn't. Though Kate's mum was all smiles and polite handshakes as we arrived, she insisted on "looking after" the various weapons being waved around by people as they arrived, probably to reduce the chances of a stray throwing star landing in the fishtank in the corner. That meant goodbye to Will and Dec's ninja gear, but also to the various guns being toted by the Idiots.

They'd dressed up as the Terminator (Matt), Neo from *The Matrix* (Keith), Blade (well, that was what Darren said, although he's white and doesn't have a moustache) and, um, the Terminator again (Nick). To be honest, I think they just wanted an excuse to wear shades and black leather jackets, although they looked a little bit forlorn without their realistic-sounding M-16s. Also confiscated was the double-headed red lightsabre (with real "vwooom" noises!) being swung around by Alquin, who'd turned up as Darth Maul – yep, with his face painted and everything. I think he'd used some sort of shower cap to get the bald-head-with-spikes effect, but he was still the most uncoordinated, shy Dark Lord of the Sith any of us had ever seen.

The only weapon not confiscated, in fact, was Rachel's lasso – well, bit of string – which she was carrying as part of her Jessie-the-cowgirl-from-*Toy-Story-2* outfit. All the It girls had dressed up as various superheroines or villainesses, which was nice (especially Hannah's Halle Berry-style Catwoman get-up) but cheating a bit (I mean, they'd obviously just bought their costumes from a shop). Kate was dressed as the Disneyfied version of *Pocohontas*, with her hair straight down and a brown dress on. OK, so it wasn't quite as spectacular as Karen's Charlie's Angels get-up, but it still looked good enough to *almost* make me wish I was dressed up as . . . well, I've forgotten the name of the bloke from *Pocohontas*. It wasn't that good anyway.

"Mind if I sit here, um . . . Daphne?" I asked, squashing myself on to the sofa. To be fair, Tamsin Townsend looked more like an aubergine than the pretty one from *Scooby-Doo*, but I didn't think it'd hurt to be polite – especially since I was trying to get back my "Nice Lad" reputation.

"Nff prbblmm," mumbled Daphne/Tamsin through a mouthful of crisps.

"Hey, Dylan," said Kate. Her smile wasn't exactly up to its usual toothpaste-ad brilliance, but I put that down to party-organization stress.

"Hi!" I said, trying to take the initiative. "Nice outfit."

Not very original, but I couldn't really think of anything else – short of launching into an off-key version of one of the songs from *Pocohontas* and hoping she joined in.

"You too," she said, not looking impressed. "Going out fighting later?"

OK, this wasn't too good.

"No. . ." I said. "I mean, I haven't been fighting at all. Well, I have, at lessons, but I don't *like* fighting . . . you know?" I trailed off, hopefully.

My bumbling attempt to explain seemed to get a half-smile out of Kate, which had to be better than nothing.

"I don't know, Dylan," she said. "I mean, I like you and everything, but sometimes you seem one way with me and then totally different when you're with your mates."

"Well. . ." I started, not really knowing what to say. She liked me? I mean, liked me like a friend, or like . . . well, how else would she like me? I mean, what if she meant. . .

"Mmmmmmf!" interrupted a muffled squeak from somewhere behind us.

It looked like Keith had discovered the one weakness in our ninja uniforms . . . which was that if you grabbed the knot at the back and pulled it hard enough, it made it really difficult to breathe. Will was clawing at the front of his hood, but the complicated arrangement of folds made it difficult to actually unravel it – and the bit of face that *was* actually exposed was going from its normal pale colour to a worrying shade of pink. The truce was definitely off.

"Pack it in, Keith!" squealed Rachel, unfortunately not doing anything about it – like, say, strangling Keith with her magic bit of gold string.

"Chhhnfff brrrrffth!" mumbled Will.

"You're suffocating him!" Rachel squealed again, starting to sound a little bit weedy for a superheroine.

"Grrrrfh fffffth!" added Will.

And it was at about that point, watching my mate's face – well, the bit I could see – go from pink to red to a slightly worrying shade of purple, that something in my head just . . . snapped. The only thing I can say in my defence is, Keith was lucky that I didn't *completely* lose it. After all, I could have just punched him in the back of the head – well, if it hadn't been for the huge crowd of witnesses. But nope, the way he was laughing, with his jaw going up and down like a cow trying to get an especially huge lump of grass down its throat, reminded me of something. So I worked out where I reckoned his mastoid muscle, that little bundle of nerves in his neck, had to be, and lined a thumb up near his neck. And *pushed*.

"Waaargh!" yelped Keith, looking like he'd just got an electric shock.

He pulled away – and, slightly unfortunately, banged his head into a wall. "Ahhh! You're dead!"

Unfortunately, it was at round about this point that I learned something important about Aiki-jitsu. See, while it's fine against people if they're shaking your hand or invading your personal space, it really isn't that much use if an angry rugby player decides to tackle you to the floor. Because that was exactly what happened next – he absolutely flattened me. Right next to the buffet table, too.

"Get . . . off!" I gasped, thrashing around while Keith tried to sit on my arms and slap me in the face.

"I'm . . . warning . . . you. . ."

I went for one more violent heave, which – unfortunately – still wasn't enough to dislodge Keith. It *was* enough to make him crack his shoulder against the living room table and hiss a bad word as a bowl of Wotsits crashed into the floor just next to my head, but that just seemed to make him angrier.

"Little . . . scumbag. . ." he huffed, grabbing something else off the table and knocking another plate to the floor in the process. "Have . . . some of . . . this!"

The next thing I knew, I couldn't see. There was a spray-can hiss, and then I had Keith's ham-sized hand in my face, rubbing what had to be the squirtable cream from the trifle in my eyes. Yet another attack that Aiki-jitsu doesn't teach a defence for.

"Off!" I shouted again, waving my arms and feeling one hand connect with a satisfying slap. And, amazingly, it worked – I felt Keith haul himself up off me, and managed to sit up, rubbing at my eyes. "Can't believe you squirted cream in my face, you. . ."

And then I stopped. Now that I could see again, it was obvious that Keith hadn't just decided to leave me alone for no reason – standing over him, looking like a completely different person from the smiley, friendly person who'd welcomed us at the door, was Kate's mum. And standing next to *her*, looking absolutely horrified, was . . . Kate.

"He started it," I mumbled, levering myself up and wincing at the crackle as I crushed another three or four Wotsits into the orange mess on the carpet. "Sorry. I'll, um, help clear up, if you like."

"Sorry," grunted Keith, and started for the door. "I'm off."

"I think *both* of you should probably leave," said Kate's mum, looking at the carnage we'd caused.

"Yeah," I said. "Sorry. Sorry, Kate."

Kate didn't say anything. She didn't even look at me.

"I'll come with you, mate," said Dec.

"Me too," piped up Will, still looking red, although now he had his ninja hood in his hand. Kate still didn't say anything as we walked to the door.

"Sorry," we all chorused again from the doorstep. "Bye."

Kate's mum shook her head, and closed the door.

"That was brilliant! Did you see the look on Keith's face? I mean, it's a pain about getting kicked out, but at least she isn't going to ring your mu—"

"Shut up, Dec," I said, without looking at him. "What time is it, Will?"

"Erm, about half-past eight," said Will, rolling up his ninja-sleeves to look at his watch. "Why?"

"Because there's plenty of time to go before the end of Aiki-jitsu," I said, still not looking at either of them. "And I'm going to go along and sort out Gary Pierce."

The Ginger Ninja

"I really don't think this is a good idea, mate," Dec huffed, struggling to keep up as I marched towards the sports centre. "I mean, you did all right against Keith and everything, but I'm not sure. . ."

"I'm not asking you to help," I muttered, not slowing down.

"I'm just *saying*," Dec protested. "That Moody bloke hates me anyway, and GP's like, teacher's pet or something, and you're going to go and. . ."

"Go, then!" I half-shouted, spinning round to look at him. "I'm not even *asking* you to come along! You've been more scared of GP than me for the past two weeks, and *I'm the one who got smacked in the eye*! Go home!"

Der-der-der-der-der-der! went Dec's phone. Everyone ignored it.

"Fine," said Dec, coldly.

"Fine," I said, even more frostily.

"I'm, um, going home as well," Will joined in. "I mean, thanks for getting Keith off me and everything, but if I get in a fight my mum's going to *kill* me. . ."

"That's OK, mate," I said. "Go."

With Dec and Will gone, I marched the rest of the way to the sports centre in silence, hoping my adrenaline wasn't going to wear off before I got there. I had a plan – sort of – but I wasn't sure it was going to work, and every step I took made me question myself a bit more. Was this really a good idea? Shouldn't I just ring my dad and get a lift home? And would Kate ever speak to me again? In fact, Keith probably did me a favour – it was only the thought of his grunting face and piggy little eyes that kept me angry enough to get to the dojo without chickening out. Even so, by the time I got to the door, I was getting a bit nervous. In fact, I might still have chickened out, if somebody hadn't taken the decision out of my hands. . .

"YA-ME!" shouted Sensei Moody, noticing me at the door. "You're a little bit late, Mr Douglas. And what *are* you dressed as?"

"Sorry, sensei," I said. "But I've just come to apologize to Gary."

There was what felt like a long, loooong pause.

"What?" said Sensei Moody.

"What?" said GP, looking like he was expecting some sort of trick.

"Well, you can probably tell I've still got a bit of a black eye," I explained, bowing and stepping on to the mat. "Because Gary punched me in the face."

"Gary?" said Sensei Moody, looking a bit confused.

"Sorry, sensei," mumbled GP, looking ashamed of himself.

"It wasn't really his fault, though," I explained, "I mean, I grabbed his shoulder *first*, so he probably thought I was invading his personal space, or something."

At this point, general mumbling broke out among the rest of the class. Sensei Moody looked like he *might* have been reconsidering teaching his punch-first-ask-questions-later philosophy. Then again, he might have just been thinking about putting me in an armlock and dragging me off the mat. I decided to make it quick.

"So, um, Gary, I'm sorry for grabbing you," I said. "And I'm sorry about the other kids from our school starting on some of the Lowfield Year Sevens the other day."

"Yeah," said Gary, looking at the floor first, then at me. "Um, sorry about your eye. And, um, sorry about my mates."

"So: mates?" I said.

"Mates," said Gary, getting up to shake my hand.

"That's lovely," said Moody, snapping out of the sort of daze he'd been in for the previous couple of minutes. "Gary – fifty press-ups. Mr Douglas – get off my mat. I've got a lesson to finish. And Gary – why were you starting fights with Dylan, anyway?"

"What?" said Gary. "I wasn't after *him*."

And then he explained everything. . .

Revenge is a Dangerous Motive...

"Brought you these," said Dec, casually lobbing a tube of Pringles at me from point-blank range.

"Cheers," I mumbled, catching them.

Neither of us are very good at apologizing – well, not to each other, anyway. It might be a lad thing, or it might be that we're just good enough mates to know that, really, the other one's sorry even if he doesn't actually say it. Whatever – at least I got some crisps out of it.

"So, um, your mum's finally realized that watching violent films isn't going to send you mental, then?" said Dec, stomping his skate-shoes on the rug.

"Yeah," I said. "And I've found a really good one. Really scary."

It was Saturday afternoon. My family were all

out – Mum going with my dad to have a much-needed post-inspectors look around the shops. Becky was upstairs with Charlie, doing . . . well, stuff I didn't like to think about. I wasn't *too* fussed, though – Becky had already helped me out with phase one of my brilliant plan, and phase two meant I needed the living room to myself.

"Erm, how'd you get on at Aiki-jitsu?" Dec asked, shrugging off his hoodie. "What'd GP say?"

"He said 'sorry'," I said, taking his skateboard and propping it up in the kitchen – where, hopefully, my mum wouldn't go *too* mental if she saw it. "He actually seemed pretty friendly."

"You must be joking!" Dec said, wandering ahead of me and pushing open the living room door. "He's an absolute lunatic! He ought to come with a government warn. . ."

There was a pause.

"Ah," said Dec.

"All right, mate?" said Gary.

He was sitting on the sofa watching Jean-Claude beat up a woman in a penguin suit. No, I'm not making that up – JC's really started to lose it in his recent films. Without even glancing at the screen, Gary flicked the video off with the remote control and stood up, nostrils flaring. I was *still* a bit scared, and I wasn't the one getting angry looks.

"Erm. . ." said Dec. "How did he get in?"

"I invited him over," I said, shutting the door behind him. "Anything you want to tell me?"

"Hang on a minute," said Dec, looking slightly panicky, even though Gary hadn't actually moved off the sofa. "You're not going to let him beat me up, are you?"

"Dunno," I said. "I hadn't really thought that far ahead. But I thought that you might have *mentioned*, y'know, that the girl you dumped the other day was. . ."

"*My sister*," finished Gary, right on cue. Dec looked as if he was thinking of making a dive for it through the living room window. I hoped he'd decide against it – all that glass would've made a complete mess of the lawn.

"Erm. . ." said Dec. ". . .Yeah. I probably should've said something about that. Sorry."

"She's been trying to speak to you for two weeks," said Gary.

"Yeah. . ." said Dec, not looking too cocky at all.

"So, what're we going to do about this? She's been pretty upset," Gary carried on, giving Dec a dismissive look, ". . .although I dunno why."

"Well," said Dec, looking very apologetic. "I suppose I *could* carry on going out with her for a bit, if you. . ."

"*No*," said Gary, very firmly. "I don't want you to carry on going out with her. I want you to apologize for acting like a little tosser."

"Yeah, I'm really sorry," said Dec, staring at a suddenly interesting patch of carpet.

"Not to me, dumbass, to *her*," said Gary, stepping closer.

"What?" said Dec. "I mean, really? You don't want. . ."

I held out the phone.

"Erm, so, yeah . . . I'm sorry," said Dec, giving Gary and me a nervous glance out of the corner of his eye as he clutched the phone to his ear. "No, yeah, *really* sorry . . . and I'm sorry I didn't reply to your. . . Yeah, I *know*. . . What, you don't really want me to *say*. . . OK, yeah, fine." He cleared his throat. "I'm a total loser. Happy now?"

He hung up – although I think I could hear a little laugh coming out of the handset as he clicked off – and gave us a defeated look. "Was that OK?"

"Well. . ." said Gary, "I think it might be nice if you sent her some flowers."

"Whatever," said Dec.

"And maybe some chocolates," I suggested.

"Don't push it," said Dec. Gary made a soft sort of growling noise, and Dec flinched. "Fine. I'll get her some Maltesers, or something."

"See?" I said, turning to Gary. "I *told* you he was a nice bloke, really."

"Yeah," said Gary, finally dropping his flared-nostrils pose and grinning at Dec. "Shake?"

Dec still looked a bit timid, as if he was expecting Gary to twist his hand off at the wrist the second he got close enough, but eventually managed a little dead-fish shake. Then we all sat on the sofa and watched Jean-Claude Van Damme beat up a penguin – and if that isn't the right way to make friends, I don't know what is.

"By the way," I said to Gary, who was shovelling Pringles into his mouth as Jean-Claude rammed the penguin's head into a steam-dryer. "You couldn't do me a massive favour, could you?"

Video Nasties

"I'll give you one-fifty for the lot," said the fat man behind the till, dismissively.

At this point, I should have put on my best gruff voice, squinted – maybe even spat on the floor – and given a little "Ha!" to show what I thought of that offer. But, as I've already mentioned, I'm not very good at pretending I'm in a film, so instead I just mumbled:

"Um, how about two hundred?"

The fat man stared at me.

"One-seventy-five."

This time I really tried – honestly I did – and I almost, *almost* managed to sound cool.

"Done," I squeaked.

Behind me, Dec and Gary breathed sighs of relief. It hadn't been easy, carting three rucksacks full of vampire/kung-fu/zombie films all the way into the town centre – even with their help – and we really hadn't wanted to have to take them all the way back home again, but hey, if you're negotiating, you've got to look like you can walk away. A hundred and seventy-five quid for Lennon's mammoth collection of B-movie tat was bad enough, but that's the problem with dealing with a second-hand shop that doesn't ask why a thirteen year old's selling a lifetime's supply of films with "Blood", "Ninja" and "Brain" in the title – there aren't that many of them around. The fat man behind the counter started counting out tenners, and I had one last mournful look at Lennon's collection. Nope, I wouldn't be watching Jean-Claude flex his Belgian muscles again in the near future, but at least my brother wouldn't have to volunteer for any medical experiments – or face the wrath of my mum – to raise some cash. Now, I just had two more things to do. . .

"Hi, Dylan," said Kate, spotting me as she wandered into the top floor of our local ultra-trendy coffee shop with a huge, frothy whipped-cream mocha in one hand. Then, as she got closer: "Wow!"

Next to me, on the sofa I'd arrived especially early just to grab, was a *massive* bunch of flowers. I'd got the nice, smiley lady at Bristol's street market to put it together for me – and got an extra-big smile when I told her what they were for.

"They aren't for me, are they?" Kate was staring at them, looking flabbergasted – if that's actually a real word. And, yeah, I seriously thought about it, just for a second – well, you would, wouldn't you? – but I had to tell the truth.

"Nope," I said. "Well, you can have some of them if you like. But they're really for your mum. To apologize for the party."

"Oh," said Kate, looking slightly deflated. "That's, um, really sweet."

"Yeah, well. . ." OK, so I felt a *bit* bad about that.

See, that was the other bit of my deal with Lennon – I'd explained it to him over the phone. I'd sell off his video collection and send him a cheque for the cash – except that he'd give me ten per cent commission for all the hassle of dragging it into town. A couple of weeks before, I'd have been terrified of even asking Kate to meet me in town, let alone being all cheeky and flirty with her. But hey – I'd been doing plenty of scary stuff recently without it fazing me too much. Even getting turned down's better than being punched in the face.

"I found out what really happened after you'd gone," Kate was saying, "so, you know, you didn't really need to get your sister to ring me up. . ."

Fine, yeah, OK, so I'd had a *bit* of help. Becky did the actual dialling and apologizing for the fight bit – I mean, with my sister in such a good mood, it seemed a shame not to get *some* use out of her.

Besides, *I* did the asking out. That was the really scary bit.

"So – still friends?" asked Kate, helping herself to a bit of my muffin.

For just a second, I had a flash of Dec saying "You're in the friendship circle" – but then, I thought, *Why not?*

"Yeah. I'll need someone to hang around with, now that I've given up on punching people," I said, sipping my latte like I imagined a wise old Buddhist monk might (although are they even allowed milk? I'll have to ask Becky).

"Really?"

"Yeah. It's too much like hard work," I said. "Anyway, as a great philosopher once said, 'revenge is a dangerous motive'."

"Oh yeah?" said Kate, fixing me with a stare. "Which philosopher said that?"

"Um," I said, trying to get a sudden flash of Jean-Claude's exposed bum-cheeks out of my head. "He's Belgian. . ."

Fortunately, I managed to forget about JCVD for the rest of the afternoon. After all, there was coffee to drink and there were bands to slag off. The time zipped by, and before I knew it, all the shops were shutting and I was standing with Kate at her bus stop, getting ready for the long walk home.

"I've had a really nice day, Dylan," said Kate, shuffling in next to a very harassed-looking mum with the most angry-looking baby I've ever seen in a pram.

"Good," I said. Then, because that didn't seem like enough, somehow. "Me too. Really, um . . . nice."

"OK, bye then," said Kate, which seemed a bit sudden, and not quite as dramatic as I'd hoped for.

"Yeah, bye," I said.

"See you."

"Yeah, see you."

"Bye."

"Bye."

This was getting a bit silly. I mumbled one last "bye" and crossed the road. *Just mates*, I kept telling myself, although it didn't seem to be helping.

"Dylan!" shouted Kate, dashing back across the road towards me. "Wait a minute!"

"What?" I said.

"I just . . . wanted to say that . . . I'm. . ." Kate gave me a look she'd never given me before – sort of dropping her face towards me and making her eyes go really wide. She looked all sort of innocent and sweet, like a baby cow. Well, a really pretty baby cow, or. . . Look, you know what I mean. ". . .I'm glad we're friends again."

And guess what I did?

If you said "kissed her," you'd be wrong.

If you said "gave her a hug', you'd *still* be wrong.

And if you said "dropped down on one knee and declared my undying love to her", you'd be *totally* wrong.

Give up?

I shook her hand.

Gnnnnngh!

Sunday Night's All Right For Fighting...

"Hit him! Make him bleed!" shouted Will.

"Not the face!" yelled Dec.

Say what you like about violence, but there's something about pounding a bloke in pyjamas senseless that really makes you feel better if you've just – for instance – blown your chances *again* with a girl you're doomed to be "friends" with. I smacked him again.

"Work the body! Stick and move! Stick and move!" shouted Will.

One more punch, and the other bloke toppled to the floor, his face looking like an extra-topping meat-feast pizza. "Player 2 Wins!" blared the screen.

"Will," I said, as Dec chucked his joypad down in disgust. "Do you even know what 'stick and move' means?"

"Erm. . ." said Will, picking up the pad and getting ready for his go.

OK, so I don't think I'll be doing any more real fighting in the foreseeable future. It's dangerous and sweaty and – although I'm glad I did it – it's a lot easier on the PlayStation 2. Will, of course, is forbidden from going near the sports centre for the foreseeable future, and Dec was never really up for all that exercise and being polite to people anyway – so as soon as he didn't have to worry about Will learning any new ways to beat him up, he left. And we won't be sneaking round to Dec's to watch *Cannibal Zombie Yakuza 4* either. After all, there has to be a time when you grow out of that sort of thing – even if you're my terminally irresponsible brother. What did he really need the money for? I'm still not sure, but the good news is that he's now fully recovered and working part-time in – *of course* – his local student pub. Hey, it gives him lots of opportunities to meet girls.

And *speaking* of girls, I still fancy Kate, of course, and maybe one day I'll work up the courage to ask her out properly – although that's a much scarier prospect than even facing down Gary Pierce – but in the meantime, there's no harm in laying a bit of friendly groundwork. In fact, the only thing that *didn't* work out OK is my relationship – if you can call it that – with Will's mum. She still doesn't approve of me, she probably never will, and as she's pointed out. . .

"I'm never normally this aggressive," said Will, picking his favourite character (it's the cute girl, natch). "I think you're a bad influence. . ."

"I've got no idea what you're talking about," I said, as "Round One" flashed up on the screen. "Now, get ready for an absolute kicking."

Don't miss Dylan's other misadventures!

Have you read:

Going Out with a Bang

"I'm not doing it," I said, in my firmest You're-Just-Wasting-Your-Time voice.

"I'm not really asking you to *do* anything, if you don't want to," pointed out Dec.

"I don't want to, and I'm not going to."

"Just come with me."

"No, because I know what's going to happen," I said, stubbornly.

After German, my mind was racing with ways to a) talk to Kate after school, b) appear much cooler/funnier/more attractive than I actually am and c) keep her away from Matt the Idiot. But then it occurred to me – there was no way I was going to do that tonight, after her first day at school. And however persistent Matt the Idiot was, it was unlikely that he was going to get to twang her bra straps, or whatever, that particular evening.

Besides, I didn't *really* know what was going to happen, whatever I told Dec. If I had, I'd definitely have walked off then and there, and not even given him a chance to talk me round. As it was, if we kept walking in the direction of the skatepark, it was only a matter of time.

Bristol skatepark's great. They might not give enough money to schools (according to my mum) or be any good at collecting bins (Dad), but there's one thing I'll say for our council – they know how to build a skatepark. A couple of years ago, they decided that something to keep The Kids out of trouble might be a good idea – and at that point they must have got some lottery money or something, because instead of just sticking a half-pipe in a children's playground, they built this enormous skate-wonderland full of grind rails, vert ramps and funboxes. On Saturdays you can sit there for ages, just watching people pull cool tricks or (even better) slam into things.

It didn't really stop the trouble, of course. The kids who used to skive off school, smoke, drink cider, spraypaint stuff and threaten other kids, didn't stop. Now they all just do it in one place, which is why all the half-pipes are covered in graffiti, the paths are all covered in crisp packets and the grass verges around the park are covered in nutters. That's why the skatepark's fine on a weekend, when there are parents around to watch their kids work on kickflips, but not exactly the greatest place to go after school. None of this matters to Dec, though. He goes there all the time – and he had a plan.

The thing is, though: I can't even skateboard. I had a go once, when I was nine, except that I'd forgotten the golden rule of any sport – if you've never tried it on flat land, *don't try it on the steepest hill in your town*. One pair of ripped trousers and two severely scraped elbows later, and that was it for me and skateboarding.

Dec's much more sensible. He can ollie things, do 50–50 grinds and manage decent manual rolls – hey, I can play Tony Hawk – they're all things he learned to do before skating was *quite* as cool as it is now. And that's enough for him. Ten minutes of serious skating and he's off wandering around and chatting to all the thrasher girls who sit on the grass banks. Which is where I was supposed to come in.

The reason he'd had to dash off on Saturday, Dec explained, was that he'd met a girl on one of his earlier trips to the park. She was really pretty, he thought he was in with a chance, and she had this mate who sort of wouldn't give them any time to themselves, and . . . and it was about that point that I worked out what was going on.

This wasn't Dec setting me up, whatever he said – it was Dec trying to get rid of someone else. And the weird thing about Dec is, he thinks you won't notice when he tries this stuff.

"Look, all you have to do is talk to Natalie's mate for a bit while we go for a walk somewhere. Otherwise I'll never get rid of her."

"Is Natalie's mate pretty?"

"Yeah! Fairly."

"What do you mean, 'fairly'?"

"I think you'll like her."

"Do *you* like her?"

"Not as much as I like Natalie."

Suddenly, I remembered our conversation in the cafe.

"Is she third division?"

"Ha! I'd say she's. . ." Dec gave it a bit of thought. "First division. Just not premier league. It's an easy away win."

"Why didn't you ask Will?"

"Because he's already been relegated."

That carried on right until we were at the skatepark. Worried as I was, I had to admit that I wanted to meet Dec's potential girlfriend – and I couldn't help wondering what her mate would be like. I probably wasn't going to fancy her as much as Kate, or anything, but there was no harm in looking, was there?

"There they are," said Dec, as we walked towards the gates.

Dec pointed at two girls lying together on one of the grass banks. They were both wearing identical black hooded tops and combats, although one of them had brown hair and the other one was blonde. I couldn't really tell what they looked like at that distance – and besides, I didn't know which one was which.

"Come on."

Before I knew it, Dec had taken his school shirt

off and stuffed it in his bag. Underneath, he was wearing a T-shirt with some sort of ultra-trendy kung-fu monkey logo on. What with that, his black school trousers and his jacket, he didn't look much different to most of the people skating. And I was still wearing my school uniform. I couldn't believe it. He'd probably been plotting this ever since that little chat in the coffee shop.

"Oh, this is great. Thanks for warning me," I said.

"It'll be fine. Come on."

"Hang on a. . . No, just stop right. . . Oh, I don't believe this." I tried to protest, but Dec was already heading straight for them.

Up closer, I started to feel even worse. Both girls were plastered with black mascara, but the blonde one was really pretty – and she was obviously Dec's type. The other one wasn't ugly, exactly, but she was really pale, had a weird smile and . . . well, she looked mad. I don't know what it was – maybe the stupid pink hair extensions, maybe the tatty, fingerless gloves or clump boots – but she just had this aura that said, Danger: Keep Away. They were both giggling at nothing in particular, except that the dangerous-looking one was making a sort of snorting noise while she did it. Eep.

"Natalie, Fiona – this is Dylan," said Dec, stepping forward with his best girl-charming smile firmly in place. Natalie, I figured out, was the blonde one, who smiled at Dec. Fiona was the crazy-looking one, who just scrunched up her nose a bit.

They stopped laughing and sat up to give me deliberately serious looks.

"Pleased to meet you."

"Nice tie."

And both of them exploded into giggles again.

I suppose I could have at least taken the tie off.

They Think it's all Over

My mate Dec has this theory.

He reckons girls can sense desperation...

"It's like football," he says. "If you haven't scored for a while, your game's off and you can't concentrate properly. The important thing's to scrape together a result against anyone, even if it's a third-division side, and get your confidence back for the cup tie. Honestly.

"Basically, Dylan, if you ever want to have a chance with someone you fancy, it might be an idea just to try getting off with someone you don't."

Dylan's not sure where this thinking will lead him but he figures he has to try *something*. That's sort of where they get the idea about Dec having a party. Party = girls = result, surely? And it would have been fine if it hadn't been for the experiment with the fireworks...

The not so Great Outdoors

"I'll give you two quid if you manage to snog Kate before the end of the week," offered Matt, generously.

"I'll make it three," added Keith.

"Look, I'm not going to bet on it..." I started.

"Will you give me three quid if I get off with Hannah?" asked Darren.

"No," said Matt and Keith, together.

"OK, how about we have a bet on who manages to snog somebody first?" suggested Dec.

"Yeah!" said Matt and Keith.

"Don't be so childish," muttered Scott.

"Shut up, Scott," said everyone who was still awake.

Dylan's not really enjoying outdoor pursuits week, but when he agrees to a *very* stupid bet he's suddenly got a lot more to worry about than sinking rafts and carnivorous bats. Even worse, there's a Mystery Prankster causing havoc in the camp and Dec seems to have gone a bit *psycho*...